DAISY

A NOVEL

LIBBY STERNBERG

Cover Design: Jaycee DeLorenzo, Sweet 'N Spicy Designs
Interior Design: TracyCopesCreative.com

Daisy Title Information
978-1-61088-587-4 (HC)
978-1-61088-588-1 (PB)
978-1-61088-589-8 (ebook)
978-1-61088-590-4 (PDF)
978-1-61088-591-1 (audio)

Published by Bancroft Press
"Books that Enlighten"
(818) 275-3061
4527 Glenwood Avenue
La Crescenta, CA 91214
www.bancroftpress.com

Printed in the United States of America

To Truman, Penny, Mina,
and Winnie

Stow the costumes, the golden hats,

The silver capes and purple plumes.

Mute your clever tunes.

Cease your acrobatic displays,

Your awful jousts and warring ways.

I want one thing, lover, one thing alone:

Tenderness.

Pamela D'Invilliers

CHAPTER ONE

Nick made a lot of money off my story. I penned the first words, and we exchanged more through letters after it was all over—a sort of game we played that helped us massage away the hurt of that wild summer and its consequences. We compared memories, filling in what each of us didn't know or had forgotten. So if you've read his version of this tale, you'll find differences in mine, some small and some significant.

You see, he'd been helping me overcome some difficulties after the tumult, and we started a long conversation by writing all about it. Then, before I knew it, the whole thing was published, first in magazines, and then as a book. He had my name on the story, too, but he was the one who received all the fame and most of the money, and eventually my name disappeared altogether from the tale, blasted away as if written in sand. So this is my chance to right that wrong, to tell it solely from my point of view, and to get credit for the telling.

The afternoon my cousin Nick Carraway came by our East Egg house, I felt as if I could fly on the gauzy breezes inhaling and exhaling our long white curtains through open doors, and I kept glancing out the window for some pure dove to invite me on a journey across the Sound.

Nick intruded on this dream as he strode into the hall trying so hard to look confident. He had this way of hesitating, sometimes in speech, sometimes in gait, just the tiniest of moments as he teetered on the edge of choosing between doing what he wanted to do or doing what he thought others expected of him.

I'd invited him after learning he lived in the less fashionable West Egg area just across Long Island Sound from us. It had been ages since I'd seen him last, and I was in need of good company. I thought of Nick that way—a good man who could see to the core of a matter. As for chosen profession, he was in bonds then, learning the trade.

Poor, dear Nick. He had tried so hard to measure up to my husband, Tom, when in reality he was Tom's superior merely by existing.

A warm wind blew wildly that day, making the curtains dance in the vast parlor that fronted the Sound and my hair a fluttering halo. I thought we were in for one of those exciting storms that sometimes rushed up the coast, whipping the house with rain and making Tom worry about trees falling and the boat going out and never coming back.

When those storms hit, I wished I could be on the boat, sailing smoothly between huge waves and torrential rain, untouched by either but finding the calm, true course in the center away from everything, and especially from Tom.

No tempests arrived, though. And Nick was ushered in by Tom, dressed in riding pants and looking like some East Indian company leader about to punish an errant dark-skinned servant.

Jordan, who was staying with us at the time, caught a glimpse of him first and immediately turned her head up and away, a habit of hers when meeting a man for the first time. Makes them nervous, she had confided to me. She also stayed quiet as a cat, another strategy of hers for causing a man to feel ill at ease, wondering if he'd inadvertently offended and then setting him on a course of talking too much, as if trying to find the precise thing that would make up for the deficiencies Jordan clearly saw in him with her silence. I could see that concern flicker across Nick's face.

Of course, she knew I had designs on setting them up together, so she was playing a role, one I'd assigned to her and she had accepted. I had the parts written in my head already, and I immediately stepped into the scene, smiling and offering a greeting. I provided some light banter about the longest day of the year – don't you always wait for it and miss it – something I'd charmed new guests with several times already, and they all thought it so original and somehow bright.

"Nick! I've missed you! Come give me a kiss and make Tom jealous!"

He did as instructed, and I could see him eyeing Jordan, so I laughed and introduced them.

"Nick Carraway, dearest cousin. Jordan Baker, dearest friend," I said, nodding to them both.

"The golfer," he said with that hesitant timidity again.

"The scandalous one, yes," Jordan said, finally bestowing on him her sweetest smile that made him think, I'm sure, they shared a secret. That was another skill of hers, making men feel they knew something only the two of them acknowledged.

Drinks and small talk followed—chatter as light as the afternoon air—and soon I floated above it all, borne on the wings of a good white wine as we went into dinner and drank and laughed some more. Tom presided at one end of the table like a grand pasha.

When Myrtle called—yes, I knew it was her—I cringed, and the bruise on my finger, where Tom had squeezed my hand so tightly he'd nearly broken a bone, began to throb.

I'd known about Myrtle Wilson for some time. I'd picked up the phone one day at the same time Tom did when she was purring at him to come visit.

I even knew she was married and lived above a garage—a garage, for God's sake. Did it make him feel as if he was doing something dangerous by cavorting with a woman of such low status?

I sometimes contemplated writing an anonymous letter to her husband alerting him to her infidelity.

Though it angered me that Tom carried on like this, I was still curious about how he had met the woman. On a trip into town, stopping by the garage? How louche!

I imagined her wearing stained dresses and sagging stockings, with a face too fleshy to be attractive.

I winced again when I heard his hushed tone, but part of me was amused by Tom, trying so hard to keep from embarrassing himself in front of our guests. Having a mistress suited him. Having it revealed in front of his wife's guests did not.

When he didn't return to the table quickly, Jordan grimaced and said, "You'd think she'd have the good taste not to call during the dinner hour."

Nick quickly turned his head to her. "Who?"

But Jordan didn't answer. And I wasn't about to mention Myrtle's name and explain who she was because I'd feel compelled to do it in a clever, amusing way to make my guests comfortable. Neither Tom nor the Wilson woman deserved such admirable treatment.

As his conversation dragged on, I had the impish desire to add to his suffering, so I wandered inside, pretending to be surprised he was still on the phone.

"Darling, if it's business, it can wait," I said. "We have guests."

His face reddened, and I made the mistake of smiling, too direct an acknowledgment of the game he was playing. Red turned to purple fury, and he slammed down the phone and came over to me. He pulled me to him, crushing me, his hand behind my neck as he forced a whiskey-flavored kiss on my lips, pushing so strong and hard I felt I couldn't breathe.

"Make them go away," he whispered, still holding on to my hair. It hurt.

I murmured something conciliatory so he would let go. But as he walked away and then poured himself another drink, I knew I would do no such thing. They'd stay until the stars crept into the black void. They'd stay until Thomas Buchanan, he of the white man's swagger, was too tired to do anything but sleep after they'd all left, or, in Jordan's case, gone up to bed.

DAISY

I think it was at that moment that a dream began to drift into my heart and mind just like that light breeze. At first, it was merely a shadow, joined by a vague outline, and not painting a full picture yet.

I remember that summer as one glorious day after another, most of them sunny and hot, but out there on our water-bordered piece of land, you could always escape into the shade and wait for ocean winds to cool your brow.

On one fine morning, I was the only one in the house other than the servants. Even little Pammy was off on a walk with her nanny and would nap soon after their return. Tom went into town, probably to see that wretched Wilson woman, and he'd taken poor Nick with him. I heard him make the arrangements over the phone. Jordan, too, left the roost, to practice, she said, at a nearby course. She came and went as she pleased, sometimes staying with other friends in town or closer to courses where she played.

I didn't often have time alone like this, with no one to tend to, no directions to give to the cook, no questions to answer about Pamela, no querulous husband to avoid, so it took me a few minutes to think of how to spend those precious hours before life intruded on my peace.

The day was once again warm, but I hungered for entertainment. I wished I could scurry into town myself to go to the cinema. We'd not been often, but I loved losing myself in those flickering stories.

I changed into linen sailor pants and a blue-striped top, grabbed my straw hat, and set out on a walk of my own. I followed an almost invisible path along the water's edge where I could enjoy the cooler salt air and see across the Sound to a mansion where nightly parties lit up the sky.

I paused at a promontory and gazed toward the jut of land where the mansion stood, somewhat hidden by towering pines and shorter maples. Nick, in his remembrances, seems to think I knew then who lived there, but I didn't. It never occurred to me to ask because one didn't envy things in our circle; we created envy, so why should I be curious about parties at the mansion across the Sound?

Still, the house intrigued me. It shouted gaiety, abandon, and un-filtered joy. With a sigh, I realized I hadn't felt those things since I was a girl on the cusp of womanhood, when summer meant effervescent happiness, filled only with potential for unbounded pleasure.

The wind shoved at the brim of my hat, and I removed it as I sat on the grass, hands around my knees, staring. I wanted something, I didn't quite know what, and I felt rather girlish.

I knew I'd been a lucky child. My doting parents would have given me the world if I'd wanted it. As it happened, I had never lacked for comforts or extravagances. Mother decorated my room in whites and golds, and Father treated me like a princess. My debutante ball took place one exquisite spring evening on the country club grounds, with nearly two hundred in attendance. I wore a dress of the purest white silk embroidered with gold thread ordered from Paris.

DAISY

I'd never wanted for beaux that summer. A parade of them sought me out at every social event I attended, and I went to many.

I didn't realize it then, but my mother had taken an egalitarian approach to my socializing. She allowed me to be courted by both wealthy heirs and lowly soldiers. With war imminent, she declared that one never knew who would be the best match. By that I took it she meant who would survive and who would flourish was out of our hands, and planning was a fool's task. I think she worried there'd simply be fewer men to choose from.

That said, she was happy when I abandoned all others and chose Tom, one of our class, maybe even above us in wealth and social status.

Truth be told, I chose him because I became deathly afraid of everything that year, and he offered a safe harbor. Afraid not just of the war, the reports of which I read with horror, but of loss more personal.

Father ultimately fell ill, was pale and distant, sometimes sitting alone in his study for hours on end. He would forget things and appear confused and distracted, so it was no surprise when Mother telegrammed to beckon me home shortly after I'd married, because Father had suffered a grievous accident.

He'd collapsed, she told me, not looking me in the eye, after tripping on the steps. He broke his neck and died instantly.

Of a woman she knew who'd just lost her husband, Mother had once observed that it was good she had married—even though it hadn't always been an agreeable marriage—and now that she was free of her husband, she could perhaps have a good life. Mother had been married to a good man, though, and they'd been happy, as far as I could tell. I think she intended that message for me, since rumors had already started about Tom's wandering eye.

Tom, I later learned, helped Mother considerably after she was forced to sell our beautiful sprawling home above the river, the one with my white-and-gold bedroom, and move to a more modest abode with just a cook and day maid. Family finances had apparently dwindled, unbeknownst to her, and that had contributed to my father's decline.

Movement at the mansion across the Sound again caught my eye. A man of indeterminate age and coloring strode to his dock, where a new two-masted cutter rhythmically kissed its moorings. The man unslipped the knots and jumped onboard with the agility of a ballet dancer. Then he hoisted the sail in smooth, muscled motions, one arm over the other, until, with a startling flap, the wind caught before he was ready. With a quick shake of his head, he corrected the error in judgment and guided the boat away from the pier's gentle waves. Warming with blush, I noticed he looked my way, and his gaze was so long and intense that I swore he was staring only at me and nothing else.

For one breathless moment, I wondered if he would sail over to me, and I shivered, both tempted and repulsed by that possibility. Ultimately, good sense won out, and I started to rise, but just as I unfurled myself, he let the wind pull him on a northerly course, and was soon gliding over the pulsing waves with a grace and speed I envied.

It was then I realized I wanted to be invited to a party at the house across the way. I wanted to get uproariously drunk and dance until dawn. I wanted to sail, as he was doing now, with nothing holding me back and only the wind ahead. I wanted to feel young again.

"Teach me how to sail," I implored Tom a few mornings later. He hadn't returned the night before, and looked hollow-eyed and in pain at this breakfast. "When we moved here, you promised you would."

He grimaced, but I knew his aching, whiskey-soaked head would make him pliable, and sure enough, he muttered a short, "All right."

"Wonderful!" I continued. "The cutter is so beautiful. It's a shame to not use it more, and I love how graceful it looks with the sheets up."

"It's a sloop," he corrected, as I knew he would. "And those are sails, Daisy, not sheets. Good god, don't you know even that?"

Of course I knew. I knew more than he did. I was an excellent swimmer and diver and longed to be on the water, but I was laying the groundwork for my request to be fulfilled, and I knew if he thought me an absolute dunderhead, he'd have to school me. Tom enjoyed feeling intellectually superior. It was one of his few pleasures these days. Like many young men, something had been cut off in him after the war. He hadn't served, and as the years went on, I think he regretted it. So many others had had their manhood tested while his had been spent on polo fields and in smoke-filled clubs.

"That's why I count on good instruction," I cooed. "If you're too busy, I'm sure we can find someone."

"No, no. I'll do it. Let's go out this afternoon."

He looked up and squinted as the maid entered the room. "Get me some bicarb, would you? I thought I'd asked already."

Before she skittered away, I asked for more coffee, which I knew she'd entered the room to serve, so I made Tom wait while she filled my cup.

The rest of our miserable meal was spent in silence.

True to his word, Tom met me at the dock at three that afternoon, the hottest time of day, and on this day, the breezes off the Sound were strangely calm. It felt as if we were holding our breath before imminent disaster arrived.

I had known it would be a difficult lesson. I'd prepared myself to be patient, to jolly him when he was snappish, to follow instructions, and to keep my mouth shut when I disagreed. I'd learned to do all that early in our marriage.

It didn't take long for me to lose my resolve, though. He'd supplied all the names of things, and explained how to tack, and how to choose the right sails, and with delight, I realized I instinctually knew how to go with the feel of the boat and not the science of sailing.

At one point, when we were dead in the water waiting for some errant wind to fill the sails, I pointed at other boats skimming by and said, "Why don't we do what they're doing?" I had seen Tom surreptitiously glancing at them, evaluating what they were doing right that we were doing wrong, so I knew this thought had also crossed his mind.

"Because I'm trying to teach you how to keep the damn boat from sinking!" He muttered a curse and mopped sweat from his brow before fixing the sails to the positions on those other sloops. Soon, we were gliding as smoothly as they were.

"No one likes a pushy woman, you know," he said after straightening out our course.

I bit my tongue to keep from pointing out he had done what I'd suggested. Men didn't like women who were right. I'd learned that early in our marriage, too. During a similar discussion a week or so ago, Tom had excessively squeezed my hand, bruising my finger. I was being too aggressive, he thought, by suggesting after dinner that maybe the white man wasn't in danger of being oppressed.

Though the first lesson was a bit nerve-wracking, it didn't dim my joy for sailing, and following that afternoon, we sailed together just three more times before I felt confident piloting the *Virginia Marie*, named after his mother, on my own. I sailed when Tom went into town, so he wouldn't know.

I sailed around the Sound, never venturing out into the wider sea, though once I was caught in a strong southerly wind and had to fight mightily to get back to our safe harbor. That incident both scared and thrilled me. So, after that, I set small challenges for myself, deliberately going out in gusty blows, even once when rain threatened. Little by little, fear gave way to confidence, and these small escapes made me feel my carefree youth returning. Even Nick, on one of his regular dinner visits, commented on how happy I was looking.

Yes, I found happiness on those afternoon excursions. I found both hard work and time to think. I loved sailing back toward our safe harbor. I loved looking up at the promontory I walked on and wondering how it would feel to dive from there into the sea. Another challenge I set for myself, perhaps on a blistering day when the water would cool my skin.

The movement of the boat made me feel as if I were moving through time, and as I bounced over each wave, a resolution hammered its way into my soul, lit by a vague dream that had started to form earlier.

Tom had to go. And so did that Wilson woman.

CHAPTER TWO

Shortly after my reunion with Nick, he betrayed me. I know he doesn't think of it that way, but what else can you call it when your cousin accompanies your husband to meet his mistress?

When Tom wandered like this—because this was now a pattern—I took a condescending attitude. Boys will be boys. It wasn't the first time a husband had strayed.

But lately, it bothered me because I began to worry that one day he'd fix on some woman who'd become more than a passing fancy. He had obligations, to me and to Pamela, and I would protect us both… if I could figure out how.

So, while he and Nick were partying in New York with Myrtle and her seedy friends and relatives, I drove myself in Tom's coupe, swathed in the softest white scarf, to meet Jordan to see a show. She was in town that day, staying with other friends as she got ready to head upstate for another tournament to play.

My attempts at matching her with Nick had met with only limited success. Or at least, no success they told me about. I knew she talked to him and had seen him for lunch in town, but little else. When I asked how things were going with him, she simply shrugged and said, "He's nice. I have fun," which told me nothing and everything. I determined to find out more during this excursion.

DAISY

I loved the city. To me, it felt as if things were always happening there.

I decided to make it my own personal holiday. I booked a room at The Plaza, met Jordan for dinner, and off we went into the sparkling dusk to some musical revue I remember little about, except lots of dancing and colorful costumes and enough comedy that my face hurt from laughing when it was over.

The city night was filled with light, from cars, marquees, streetlamps, and the symmetrical rectangles of windows, where a thousand eyes peered at us from above. Those artificial stars would have to do. The real ones dimmed amidst all that light, as if allowing these pretend-cousins their chance to shine.

Though the weather wasn't oppressive yet, the theater was warm, and once the show started, the two huge fans on either side of the stage were cut off so we could all hear the players.

The hall became a sauna, and I regretted wearing my blue jersey dress, for it clung to me like syrup, despite fanning myself with my program for the entire performance.

"I think I lost several pounds in there," Jordan said as we made our way past the crowd into the cooler air outside the theater after the show. "I'd forgotten why I never go to the theater in summer."

"Oh, it was divine," I gushed, still happy from the laughter, fun, and sheer brightness of it all. Sometimes, I felt like a squire's wife out in East Egg, leading a quiet life while others enjoyed "the season" in town. After the first exciting honeymoon days, I'd frequently felt that way. Tom seemed to prefer us both at home. Or me, at least.

"We need a cold drink," Jordan said, stepping forward to hail a taxi. "Do you know a place?"

She looked at me as if I were a child on her first outing into the big city.

"I know just the place," she said as a cab pulled up to the curb.

Once inside, she gave the driver the address of a speakeasy—some new place on Bedford Street she'd heard was good.

At our destination, she paid the driver. And then we were making our way into the smoky interior, crammed with people, a jazz group playing in the corner, more excitement and fun, overlaying a sense of Prohibition naughtiness. We were disobedient children, up to impish fun.

"Here!" Jordan announced as she grabbed a table two lonely hearts had just vacated.

"What if they're coming back?" I said as we slid slowly into the chairs.

"Well, they aren't. Not when someone's at their table!" she shouted over the hubbub.

Soon we had ordered and downed iced gin cocktails and laughed at how we each felt like limp rags.

"Or wet dogs," Jordan said, pushing a strand of hair from my face. I couldn't bring myself to look in my compact. I must have been quite a sight—dress clinging to me in the wrong places, damp hair plastered on my head.

"Woof, woof!" I countered.

"It doesn't really matter here," Jordan observed, as she lit a cigarette. "They must have imported this fog direct from London, and I'm sure we look like gauzy nymphs, all a blur, like in French paintings."

I lit a cigarette, too, and we enjoyed the music along with the sense that we were doing something mischievous and decadent. "What'll I do when you are far away?" some nasal-voiced singer bleated out.

"How is Nick?" I asked, keeping my promise to myself to find out more about their romance.

Her mouth quirked into a lopsided grin. "He's fine. But you probably know more than I do. He's your cousin."

"Aren't you still seeing each other?" I prodded.

She paused after our second round of drinks came and took a drag from her cigarette. "We see each other," she said. "But he has someone else."

My eyes widened. Timid Nick a double-timer? Oh, no. Had he followed my husband's example? I felt sick.

Seeing my distress, Jordan went on. "Not someone he's seeing. It's a girl he left behind, out in California somewhere. She must have thought they'd marry. I don't like worrying if she'll show up bent on avenging their true love."

At that, I smiled. I knew, from talking to Nick before he came to dinner, that he had broken off with a girl out west. He must have told

Jordan the story, too, which made me wonder just how over the girl he was. Jordan was no fool, so I didn't blame her for being cautious.

"Has he invited you to tea?" she asked.

"No, why? Was he supposed to?"

She shrugged. "He mentioned to me that he wanted you to see his place."

After that brief exchange, the gin began to lift the heat and vexation off me. I had just about worked up my courage to go powder my nose and see what damage the hot theater had wrought when a familiar figure walked by—a broad-shouldered, long-faced man, not a hair out of place, in a tan, unwrinkled flannel suit. At first, I couldn't believe who it was, and I stared at him at length until Jordan inquired if he was a gangster or someone on a Wanted poster.

"Edouard?" I said as he strode toward the bar. He turned. Yes, it was him, and my heart gave a little leap, even as my hand fluttered to my sweat-dampened hair.

He looked at me as if he didn't recognize me, at which point I wished I'd made that trip to powder my nose earlier. When I'd known him, I was always well-dressed and well-coiffed and felt like the loveliest woman alive.

He, of course, was stunning; his blue eyes fixed on me as the corners of his sensual lips rose in an amused smile. At last, recognition seemed to dawn and he came over to our table.

"Cherie, is it you?" He leaned down and kissed me on both cheeks, and then I introduced him to Jordan.

"This is Edouard Janvier," I said. "He flies airplanes. Tom and I met him in Paris last year when we did the Tour."

Another man Tom felt inferior to, Edouard had been an aviator during the war and went on to start an airplane company. We'd met at a tea at some Frenchwoman's apartment, an acquaintance of Tom's family or something. It was a rococo flat with lots of cake frosting decorations on the ceiling and walls, and it felt so silly and formal when just outside the city were charred fields, lonely graveyards, and utter destruction.

I'd been horrified when Tom and I had taken a drive through the countryside. Tom, by contrast, had seemed unmoved, or at least stone-faced with resentment, muttering "What a waste" when I knew he secretly wished he'd been part of it, now that it was safely over.

Edouard had been there. If he had great charm, he also exuded great sorrow, and his eyes held a sadness that no smile could hide.

He had charmed me with his broken English and formal manners, and his refusal to joke about those battlefield horrors. He'd scolded Tom for making light of something related to the war with a quick question: *Avec quel regiment avez-vous servi?*

He told me he was impoverished royalty, that his father or father's father had been a duke or maybe an earl, or perhaps they had just been peasants, but he never knew because he was raised by nuns after being orphaned. It had been a sweet and sad story, and I knew parts of it were an exaggeration, but his war record was not. We encountered several people who spoke of him with awe when I mentioned meeting him. Later, we danced at someone else's house, on the veranda, a waltz, and at the end of it, he kissed me, pulling me to him as if he couldn't resist me, his strong warrior hand on my back, his chest against mine, his wine-scented breath on my face.

I could have been his lover. He sent notes and flowers, and when Tom flitted off to ride horses with some old chums, I had the time and opportunity to take Edouard to my bed. But after a sunlit afternoon of drinks and strolling, holding hands, and sipping orange-flavored liqueur at an outdoor café, I ultimately kissed him goodbye. I was still devoted to my marriage then.

"Let me introduce you to my wife," he now said, and before us stood a stunning brunette, with dark eyes and dark wavy hair she'd pinned at her nape to appear as if she had a bob. From every man in the room, she drew admiring looks. She wore a dark maroon dress that, with her hair and eyes, made her smooth porcelain skin all the more luminous. She was easily the most beautiful woman in the room.

"Patrice, this is…I'm sorry, but I have forgotten your married name." He smiled more broadly, but I recognized the lie, and a deep disappointment draped over me. He'd forgotten my entire name, not just the Buchanan part. My face warmed anew, and I knew I now sported a red glow that probably added a feverish glaze to my swamp-rat look.

"Daisy Buchanan," I said to the two of them. "Edouard and I met in Paris last year."

Patrice nodded, smiled, and said something to him in French. Though I couldn't quite catch it, I knew enough of the language to make out her question: Was I one of his "romances?" She said it in a light and breezy way, as if amused and unthreatened by his past, and he responded with a vigorous, "*Mais non, non,*" that humiliated me afresh.

"So nice to see you again," he said to me. "You look well."

I looked anything but, and his easy lies made me wonder how many of them I'd accepted as truth a year earlier, not just the fantastic stories of his childhood but his claims of devotion to me.

"And you," I said. "Don't let us keep you. It's a madhouse here." I waved him off, as if dismissing him, and this restored a little of my dignity, to be able to push him away. Again. I swallowed my disappointment.

Excusing himself to go to the bar, he put his arm lightly on his wife's back to usher her safely through the crowd. As they stood waiting for their drinks, she leaned her head onto his shoulder. He glanced at her with a loving smile before kissing her thick hair. The gesture made me feel jealous.

"Tell all," Jordan said, catching my gaze. "Leave nothing out."

"He was a friend. That's all."

She barked out a laugh.

"If I'd wanted more, it could have been more, but I didn't." I nodded my head as I said this to emphasize I had been the one rejecting him.

She opened her mouth to comment but tactfully closed it before uttering a word. I could have provided the words myself. *He certainly didn't look like he'd wanted it to be more. Why, he barely remembered you.*

After that, I did make that trip to powder my nose, and was relieved to see I didn't look as bad as I thought. After a quick splash of water on my face, some powder, a comb through my hair, and a straightening of my dress, I felt my old self again, pretty and confident, and strode back into the room, ready to make every woman envious.

It was too late, however. Edouard and his bride had left.

When I sat down again, Jordan leaned forward. "You shouldn't hold yourself back, dear…if you want to take a lover, that is. Men do it all the time."

She knew about Tom and never seemed as upset about his affairs as I was. She accepted his behavior as the way of the world.

"I don't think I could," I said. "It takes up so much of one's time."

She laughed again. "Too much time or too much…courage?"

I frowned with irritation. I was a bold girl, always one to take risks and show both beaux and belles alike that I could swim farther, dive deeper, drive faster than anyone else.

"Not courage," I countered. "The opposite. I think it takes more bravery to make a go of things."

Jordan shook her head. "To what end? So you can both feel equally miserable?"

"Jordan!" I sat back. "Is that what you think marriage is?"

She didn't hesitate. "To some… and for no good reason, if you ask me." She leaned forward. "Keep your heart open to love, Daisy. I know you miss it."

The music got louder, and our conversation ceased. It was just as well. Her words made me uncomfortable. Did she think I was a coward for not following Tom's example? Did she think him a good example to follow? Was I the fool and Tom the wise one?

We stayed only a half hour longer, when I begged off, complaining of a headache.

Like a prophecy, it came true. My head was pounding by the time I crawled into bed after a soothing bath, downing a glass of bicarb and reading the latest copy of Vanity Fair.

In the morning, I awoke refreshed but troubled, and I ate breakfast alone in my room trying to figure out what vexed me so.

It wasn't that Edouard had married.

It wasn't even that he'd married such a beautiful girl.

It was that I had not occupied as great a place in his memory as he occupied in mine.

I stood and paced to the window, cigarette in hand. Perhaps all my memories of infatuated suitors were similarly false. In my fairy tale youth, perhaps I'd just imagined being more popular than I had actually been, and I began perusing my past for evidence that I'd not been fooled by a conspiracy of friends in order to mock me behind my back.

Once, at a country club dance, one of the girls' fathers came over to me with a box of long-stemmed roses. I smiled and said, "For me?" as I reached out for the gift.

"Oh, just one. They're for all the girls," he said. Somewhat surprised, I flushed with embarrassment, made a joke of it, and took one rose.

Now I wondered if I'd thought of my beaux that way—as a carton of roses just for me when that wasn't the case at all.

No, no, no. I shook my head, remembering: the many dance partners, the constant stream of callers, the men who tried to impress me with their athletic prowess, their daring, their looks, their money.

That hadn't been a dream.

Even Edouard's attentions hadn't been a fabrication. Perhaps he was a gigolo. Perhaps he'd forsake his wife at some point. But when he'd paid attention to me, he had been my gigolo, and I became the one to forsake him.

This soothed me, and I moved on to the other thought that troubled me—Jordan's suggestion that I needn't be as faithful as I thought married couples should be.

You must not think I was a paragon of virtue. No, it was more that I loathed self-righteousness. I particularly despised religious leaders urging temperance in the most intemperate of tones. I despised hypocrisy, and that's what bothered me about Jordan's idea.

If I thought Tom was wrong for his adultery, how could I then turn around and engage in the same behavior without being a hypocrite?

Maybe that was all that was holding me back, though. It wasn't that I clung to some unrealistic ideal of a perfect marriage, one where each spouse was as passionately in love years after the wedding as they were on the day itself. But I did cling to some small romantic notions, such as keeping one's promise to stay true. I suppose I thought if you managed that single accomplishment, maybe the bigger romantic picture would become real, that the original passion would return, and you could once again revel in the warm, sweet days of first love.

I balled my fists as I thought about this, feeling once again as if I were a naïve fool. Tom would likely never return to faithfulness now that he knew he could sin with impunity. Ever since he had first strayed, I'd wondered if I should divorce him, take Pamela with me, and go far away… maybe even find another man who would stay true.

Marriage to the right man had been what had given me meaning in life. It had been the goal of every girl I knew. Once I attained it, though, any sense of greater purpose evaporated, and I felt adrift, constantly looking for things that would replace that original aim. Motherhood had briefly filled the space, but mothering was such an ongoing constant in my life it hardly felt like a goal. It was too easy. I needed something to strive for, something difficult. Maybe I had made fidelity that "something difficult."

Jordan's suggestion, however, was that I just accept marital affairs as part of marriage, that instead of waiting for Tom to change his ways, I should change mine.

What kind of life would that be? Could I be happy then?

I'd pondered these questions before, and had no answers, just as I had none now, so I finished packing up and left.

After a morning spent shopping, I then drove back home, enjoying the solitude in the car, the sense that I was in charge.

When I arrived, Tom was still away, but the maid told me that Mr. Carraway had called.

"Did he leave a message?" I asked, handing her my bag, gloves, and hat.

"No, ma'am. He said he would try again if he hadn't heard back from you."

With a puzzled frown, I started up the stairs, then stopped and called down to her.

"Tell Cook that Pamela and I will have dinner in my room tonight. Just something light. If Mr. Buchanan returns, tell him we're not feeling well."

Tom didn't return that night, but Nick did call again, just an hour after I'd changed and unpacked. After some breezy chatter about the show I'd seen in town, he got to his point.

"I'd like to invite you to tea," he said. "To show you my place. You would like to see it, wouldn't you?"

"It's my life's goal," I teased. So here was Nick's tea invitation, the one Jordan had mentioned. I wondered if they were conspiring behind my back.

"Wonderful! I'd hoped it was," he responded.

"You realize, though, you mustn't disappoint me. I expect nothing less than service as if I were Queen. I've always wanted to be a queen. Or at least a princess."

"You are, though, most definitely. The Queen of East Egg," he said. Then, after a pause, "But don't bring your king. Just you."

"What king?" I replied. "This monarchy has but one ruler, and it is I, a woman!"

He laughed, and I went on: "Why not bring Tom? You're not going to kidnap me and ship me to some savage country, are you?"

"Oh, dear, you've discovered my plan." But after another pause, he said, "I just thought it might be nice to…to see you alone. We are family after all."

It seemed odd, but I liked a mystery. Besides, after my encounter with Edouard, my spirits needed lifting, and maybe a gossipy afternoon with Nick would be just the ticket.

"Name the day and hour, and I'll have my carriage at the ready," I said.

CHAPTER THREE

Nick tricked me.

Later, I found out Jordan had been in on the ruse, that she'd reached out to Nick to set all this up, this crazy romantic scheme. She knew of it the night she and I had drinks together, when she talked of infidelity as if it were part of the marriage vows.

The clues presented themselves immediately. As I walked up to his door, the scent of flowers was so overpowering that I wondered if he'd spilled some particularly poorly chosen cologne before my arrival. Rain seemed to amplify the smell, or maybe it was the umbrella acting as some sort of megaphone for rich perfumes.

Working out the details for this "tea," I had suggested another day, but Nick had insisted on this one. When I pressed him for a reason, he replied with vagueness, mentioning something about perhaps getting a closer look at his neighbor's manse, where all the festivities regularly occurred—he knew I was curious—and how this day was the best for his schedule because he was a working man, after all.

He'd repeated that I should come alone.

I'd begun to think he had some family issue he needed to discuss in private, and I imagined spending a pleasant hour sipping tea and eating sandwiches, hearing about some decrepit uncle or imprisoned third cousin, and we'd decide whether we should help him out or let him rot.

I even started looking forward to it. Before I married, I often had gossipy afternoons with girl friends, and I thought I'd come away from this encounter with some interesting dinner talk to amuse Tom with, stories of Nick's work, or maybe even a war tale or two.

Now, as I walked toward the door, I had an odd sensation that something was off, something I hadn't imagined or couldn't even imagine. Perhaps this was the kind of fairy tale about ogres and monsters rather than princes and granted wishes. I became afraid, wondering if I should have sent the chauffeur away so soon. The quick patter of raindrops. The overpowering scent of flowers. My footsteps softly clicking on the stone path. The door ajar.

"Daisy, come in, come in," Nick said nervously in the shadows. He disappeared as he opened the door more fully, revealing another man, standing with his hands clenching and unclenching by his side, nervous as a pony about to start its first trot around the track.

I couldn't see his face, just the fine cut of an expensive white flannel suit with wide lapels, cuffed pants, crisp silver shirt, which seemed to shine like a beacon in the dim interior.

I approached, unsure of this surprise, now wondering how well I really knew my cousin and if his work had taken him into dark alleyways and evil intentions, if my joke about kidnapping had cut too close to the truth. I couldn't seem to stop, though. As I neared the house, just ten feet away now, the man's features came into focus.

I inhaled sharply and, on the cusp of leaving, halted, but how could I leave? Not now, not when I saw before me a relic of my past. Him.

Rain beat against my umbrella. I stood still, unable to move forward or back. This man...

This man who almost caused me to abort my wedding to Tom with a letter that scorched my soul.

This man...

As suddenly as it started, the rain stopped. It left a strange silence punctuated only by the thrum of water through a roof gutter and a brave chirp from a faraway bird.

I couldn't move. I couldn't even blink.

"Daisy?" He said it so softly that for a moment I wondered if he'd really spoken at all or if I had imagined the running water somehow pulsing out my name. "Why—why are you alone?" he asked as if he'd rehearsed it.

I felt a giggle rise in my throat. The first thing he'd said to me when we first met. The giggle would have turned into a sob if I didn't act, so I moved forward.

As if in a slow procession, I propelled myself through the door, hypnotized, wanting to ask this ghost so many questions about what had happened to him.

Jay Gatsby.

I'd not known him by that name before he went to war. I'd known him as one of my sweetest and most ardent suitors, the one I might have married had the war not carried him away and Father's change in mood had not sent me into a paralyzing spiral of fear.

He'd been one of those who'd stolen kisses from me, sometimes even on our front porch on warm evenings as golden as those here on the Sound. He'd been the one who'd charmed me—and Mother—with his talk of moving up in the world, of making something of himself.

The eagerness that had shone in his eyes—my, it took one's breath away. You believed everything he said, and his desire for me wasn't the same kind other boys bestowed on me—a combination of lust and awe and envy and pure greed that I'd come to accept as expected.

His was pure, a simple, driving longing to have what he wanted, and what he wanted was beauty and love and tenderness.

The same as me.

For a while, he had seemed like the only man in the world, and I his Eve. For a while…

"Oh…oh…" was all I could muster, and there was the same sweet hesitation from him, not borne of timidity but of affection. He wouldn't make a move without my approval.

It was as if we had spent our lives waiting for this moment. I hadn't realized I'd been waiting, but now I knew why I'd been so desperately unhappy. It was him. I had been aching for him.

For several long seconds, we just stood across from each other and stared, me on the threshold, him by the settee, surrounded by a dozen funerals' worth of flowers, tea sandwiches and pastries on a polished silver tray wilting in the greenhouse atmosphere.

At some point, Nick must have taken my dripping umbrella and excused himself because all I knew was that I was suddenly alone with a man I'd been deeply in love with years ago.

"Daisy," he breathed out, and I closed my eyes and remembered him whispering my name, as if it were a supplication to the heavens, and all he asked for was my favor. "Daisy."

Truth be told, I never liked my name. The daisy is not a distinguished flower, and though it's associated with a bright youthful sunniness I hoped I embodied, I wished I had been called something more romantic, less quotidian. Lenore, perhaps, or even Elizabeth or Beatrice, a name one could envision men fighting for.

But when Jay Gatsby said it, Daisy sounded like the only name on earth worth having, and I could imagine a ballroom full of women looking up and envying the girl announced with that moniker.

"Daisy."

As if in a dream, I walked over to him and was about to let him embrace me—I saw his hands begin to move up and out—when lamplight caught my wedding ring, and a dancing glimmer of its reflected sparkle flashed a warning. I was married.

"Jay?" I said and sat in a chair across from the settee, the tea items spread between us like a chaperoning matron. "I didn't realize…"

I didn't realize it had been his house, his parties, his sailboat. I didn't realize he'd become everything I'd wanted before marrying Tom—comfort, security, love, joy, and, yes, even money.

DAISY

I didn't know whether to laugh or cry, to curse Nick or to thank him for setting up this rendezvous.

For the first time, I felt unsure of myself around a man. In my debutante days, I was always the one to put the fellow at ease. I was the one who enjoyed watching them preen and bow, flatter and twitch. I was never nervous, never at a loss for words.

Yet now I sat mute, a tentative smile on my face as I thought what I should say, if I looked all right, if the breeze had tousled my hair too much, if I'd sufficiently covered a blemish on my cheek with powder, if I'd applied too much rouge.

I was still smarting from my reunion with Edouard, and now I wondered if this, too, would lead to humiliation in some way, if I was being set up for disillusionment.

I thought of leaving, but instead I sat like a schoolgirl, legs crossed at my ankles, back straight as a board, hands demurely in my lap, and I nodded and listened. Or tried to listen. Jay was telling me of the war, how hard it had been, how he'd lost good friends, how he'd come out of it with two goals in mind—never to waste a day, and to live the life he wanted, no matter how difficult it was to attain.

"Daisy?"

He had asked me a question, and I'd not heard it. Instead, I was lost in that question that plagues so many after a certain time: *What if?*

"Yes?" I asked and smiled, drifting back to an earlier time.

Jay in his brown uniform, looking as if it were a size too big, his right cheek raw from a close shave, his straw-colored hair, as always, in need of a brush, or the stroke of my hand over a boyish cowlick that would never stay down.

Jay laughing at some silly thing I'd said, sipping lemonade on my porch, the sun angling across the land as if aiming right for us, turning us both golden with its rays.

Jay taking me in his arms the night before he was to ship out and telling me he'd always be true, and would I wait for him? Yes, he knew I would. He knew I would wait.

"Are you happy?" he asked simply, his brows coming together. He knew that was a hard question to put to someone.

"Very happy, thank you." I said it simply and quickly, just as I would have, had I been meeting with any old acquaintance. "Tom and I have a daughter, a beautiful little girl, and he bought this house—the one across the bay—when business brought him to New York more and more, and it's so lovely being here, so many things to do, especially in the city, and I absolutely love where we are, close to everything but far enough away to breathe, and…and… and I'm very happy, so happy…"

I bowed my head, bit my lip, and could not stop the tear that fell onto my gloved hands. The lie had torn me open.

He saw, and in an instant was by my side, kneeling before me, holding my hands.

"Oh, Daisy. Has it been hard on you?"

I couldn't speak. I just nodded, and then he folded me into his arms. I had forgotten how muscular they were, and I cursed the gods for splitting us apart because of war. He dabbed at my eyes with a handkerchief of the softest silk, and we stayed there, though it must have become frightfully uncomfortable for him on the floor beside me. Yet, I knew that if we moved, it would only be even closer toward each other, and that had to be a conscious decision, not a hastily made choice when I was emotionally fraught.

At long last, a clock chimed, serving as the cue for us to part, so he stood, quick and careful, and pointed to the tea.

"Here, let me get you some," he said, acting the servant as he poured me a cup. "Wish we had something stronger."

He handed me the tea with a steady hand, though mine shook enough to make the cup rattle in the saucer, a beautiful china set I couldn't imagine Nick owning. I usually took a dot of sugar in my tea, but I couldn't bring myself to reach for it, too afraid I would spill my serving and embarrass myself even further.

The tea was the right choice, however, and after a few calming sips, I regained my composure enough to engage in real conversation.

"This is a good time to run into you," I now said, affecting the light, teasing tone of my younger days. "I'm at a point where I need to get out more. With the move, we've not done much socializing except for family. Nick, you know, is my cousin. So it will be good to get to know more people. We have the most beautiful house—not as large as yours, of course—but a perfect setting for entertaining."

"I do a fair amount of that," he said, and I detected in his voice an eagerness blended with amusement. The very attitude I'd always had when entertaining suitors.

"So I've heard."

"Then you'll have to come to one of my parties. I throw one almost every night. Everyone comes. Show people, judges, stockbrokers, even a classical pianist or two."

"Sounds lovely."

"I enjoy the parade of them. I enjoy learning things I didn't know." Now he was back to his old self, the striving joyfulness that attracted me. The vast openness that assumed you'd not judge him for being ignorant as long as he strove to learn more.

After that, our conversation flowed with ease. I even managed to nibble at one of the watercress sandwiches, while he downed several, plus cucumber toast and petit fours galore.

We talked about people we had known, and I was distressed to hear of even more war deaths than I'd previously been aware of. We talked of my father's passing, my mother's worsened circumstances—I made sure to credit Tom for helping her financially—and my new love of sailing.

"We'll have to go out together. I've got a fine big boat," he said.

"I know. I saw you." Warming, I looked down. I shouldn't have let him know.

"Well then, it's decided." And with a clap of his hands, like a boy who'd just opened a present, he said, "Tomorrow at one? I could sail over to get you."

"No, no. I…" I was about to refuse, but I thought of the boat, the water, the sense of freedom it gave me, and I realized that this was what I wanted right now, more than a party, more, in fact, than anything else. "I'll come to you. I'll sail to Nick's little dock and see him, then walk over."

The perfect excuse, one of many I was to make in the coming weeks.

Then Nick reappeared and Jay suggested we look at his house. Of course I wanted to see it. I wanted to know how he lived.

The rain stopped, and Nick said he didn't need to come with us, but I insisted because I didn't want to be alone in Jay's big place with only Jay. I was afraid. Of myself.

Room after room of Versailles-like splendor, a library full of books no one could read in a lifetime, artworks I recognized as belonging in a museum. His suite was the most wonderful of all, not something big and grand, but lovely little rooms, and a gold hairbrush on his dresser so attractive I couldn't resist running it through my own coiffure.

He seemed extravagantly pleased that I was pleased, and it touched me and saddened me all at once. It seemed he had stored all of this up for me, as if it were a huge gift he'd waited five years to present.

He opened his closet to reveal shelves of neatly folded colorful shirts and began to laugh and throw them onto the floor. I laughed, too, and picked one up, and then I cried because it was so beautiful. He so much needed me to say it was beautiful, and I felt, when presented with this great, awful gift of enduring love, I didn't know if I was worthy of it.

I felt inadequate, as if I couldn't muster enough gratitude for this stunning display. As if I couldn't sufficiently demonstrate how happy

I was for him, and for us that we'd found each other again. I ached with inadequacy.

When we finally walked out into the steaming sunlight, I felt wilted and old, as if seeing myself from a time far in the future, looking back at what I could have had. Here was that romantic ideal I'd held in my heart, a love who had stayed true.

I should have waited for him.

INTERLUDE
1917

I didn't want to go. The dance was a big patriotic event put together by Louisville mothers to honor the boys about to go "over there," but I hated pretending.

I thought it a foolish war, and even more foolish to celebrate it with a dance. Though I was only a young girl with no understanding of the world, I did comprehend one simple fact—that this particular war wouldn't be over until one side had let enough men sacrifice themselves on the altar of Mars. Somehow, I knew that adding American soldiers to that pile would tip the odds in our side's favor but at the cost of thousands of lives. That's how I saw it: a huge pile of soldiers, and whichever side had the bigger pile won, because they wouldn't run out before everything was all over.

It seemed like such a waste, and I will admit that back then, part of my anger and disgust was very personal. I knew the number of eligible men would diminish, meaning I'd have fewer choices.

I was courted by many. Dozens of beaux sought me out at dances and teas, croquet parties, polo matches, and strolls along the Ohio River where some stole kisses. Others were too timorous to even hold my hand.

So far, though, only a few men interested me enough to trigger daydreams of walking down the aisle with them. One was Rupert Templeton, a tall, lanky redhead with a penchant for reciting poetry. His poor eyesight was keeping him out of combat, but he still signed up to do some cartography and other desk-bound jobs. I liked his bookishness and dreaminess.

A more amorous beau was a man named Andrew Cash, and despite his last name, he was a poor New York soldier whose family owned a bakery. It wasn't his poverty that made me think twice, though. It was that he was a Catholic. My parents would never tolerate that match, and I spent many hours wondering if that was why I found him attractive—he was forbidden fruit, and I always felt delightfully rebellious whenever I saw him.

Neither of these men, nor the parade of others who tried to win me over, had me swooning the way some of my friends did over their beaux. Malvern Haskell, one of my best friends at the time, talked only of her fiancé, Dewitt. And Helen Beaufort canceled all long-made plans to go out with her beau, Theodore Clarkson. I'd long ago stopped counting on her as a friend.

So I was angry at everyone—at my girlfriends for abandoning me for their gentlemen, at the war for simultaneously placing so many men within reach to tease me when fate might snatch them away in an instant, and at my own heart for never lighting up with anything but mild interest. I wondered if there was something wrong with me.

"Daisy, dear, are you getting ready?" My mother knocked lightly at my bedroom door and I rose from the bed where I'd been looking through a fashion magazine. Still in my robe, I opened the door.

"I'm not feeling well," I said. "I want to stay home."

She immediately held her fingers to my brow. "You're not warm. Your color is good, and you took a drive with your friends earlier, didn't you?"

Yes, I had. My mother knew me too well. I turned and went back to my bed, sinking into its soft surface, hands in my lap.

"I don't want to go. I think the whole thing is silly, and I don't want to be part of it."

Mother walked over to me and sat beside me.

"Yes, it is silly, and I know it is hard to take part in something one doesn't believe in. But these boys are leaving soon, and it will do them good to see some pretty girls before they head out. Think of it as doing them a favor," she said softly. That musical voice of hers went up and down ever so slightly, making you want to listen to her forever.

"You can wear your pink chiffon," she went on when I didn't respond, "and stay just an hour, just long enough to smile and talk for a bit. You can say you're needed at home and must leave early. Your father can pick you up at eight."

"Tell a lie?" I asked, giggling.

My mother wrapped an arm around my shoulders and kissed me on the temple.

"It's not a lie. I always need you at home," she said. "You brighten my days." Then she hugged me and kissed me again on the forehead. "Here," she said, standing up, "let me get your dress."

Knowing I had to stay only an hour, I quickly slipped into my pink garment. I favored simple clothes—I still do—with clean lines and no frills. This dress was a recent acquisition, bought at a New York house and altered by a local seamstress. It had a straight neckline and long transparent sleeves in filmy chiffon, an overlay of the same fabric that stopped a foot above the hem of the satin cloth underneath. The original design had a two-inch fringe of black thread at the overlay hem, but I'd had the seamstress remove that and a matching fringe collar, as well as the wide satin belt. Instead, it barely cinched my waist with a gold cord. I wore it with the thinnest gold necklace and a lapis lazuli teardrop pendant. I loved pairing deep hues with lighter ones.

It was warm that night, so I didn't bother with a wrap. Father drove me to the country club in our Model T, as if he were my chauffeur. He loved to drive.

Before getting out, I gave him a peck on the cheek. As he rumbled away, I went up the steps to a wide porch circling the huge building. Already I could hear music from within, a dance tune with flutes and violins.

The place was awash in flags, and the patriotic theme continued to the food tables, where a red berry punch bowl sat in a plate piled with blueberries and white frosted pastries. Red napkins sat next to blue plates and white cups. As I helped myself to the confection, I wondered where they came by it all.

I waved to some friends across the room, and when they came to talk to me, I told them of a fierce headache I was battling. "I doubt I'll stay long," I said.

"But you're so good to show up when you're not feeling well," Candace said, squeezing my arm. She wore one of those fringed dresses so popular at the time, which made me glad I'd had them removed from my own frock.

"You look divine, though," Lilith remarked, squinting at me. She usually wore glasses but had removed them for the occasion. "Are you going to bob your hair?"

We'd all talked about it—getting our hair cut short—and Lilith had pioneered the look in our group. She had thick dark hair, almost black, and the style enhanced her pixie-like features, but I wasn't sure yet if it was for me. I had pinned my wavy locks at my neck, letting a few tendrils free.

"Not yet, Lil. Maybe I'll do it once my soldier goes off to war," I teased.

"What soldier?" Candace asked. "Andrew or Rupert? Or are you seeing someone new?" She always kept track of the boys, as if those of us who had two or more callers were hoarding them somehow.

"Neither. Someone new. I haven't met him yet."

They laughed. "Maybe you'll meet him tonight." Then she added, "I don't think you're ever going to bob your hair, Daisy. I think you just say that to keep us all interested."

Candace could be such a prissy thing, tallying up boys and pointing out our "lines."

"Well, then, I'm successful if you've remembered how many times I say it. You're interested," I countered. "You'll be the first to know when I cut it!"

I excused myself after that and wandered outside, sitting on one of the long wicker couches. I was the only one there enjoying the dusk, listening to the music and laughter, thinking that I could soon go home and stop the pretending. I'd heard they might auction off dances. I cringed at the thought.

"Why are you all alone?" His voice came to me before he appeared because he was climbing the steps to the porch, hidden behind a massive boxwood. At first, I thought he was addressing someone else. It was a rude question, after all, but then he appeared, broad-shouldered in a brown uniform, hair ruffled from the breeze, his hat in his hand, and a huge open smile on his face. His question hadn't been a mark of discourtesy. He was being frank.

"Why are you so late?" I said.

"My car broke down," he said. "It's actually not mine exactly. Some of us went in on it so we could get around when we wanted to. It's a bright red touring car, but it doesn't like to start in rainy weather."

"It's not raining," I said, and liked how he just went on unabashedly telling me every detail, as if we'd known each other for ages.

"Oh, yes, I know. It rained yesterday, though, and that seemed to be enough to set her back on her heels. I think she's a woman. Kind of temperamental."

By then, he'd reached the porch and come over to me. Without waiting for an invitation, he sat down next to me, and I was ready to take offense when he immediately scooted away a few inches, as if realizing he had taken a liberty. He leaned forward, holding his hat between his knees.

"Where are your friends?" I asked. "The ones you bought the car with?"

"Oh, I didn't buy it. I fixed it. I'm good at that, so I get to use it pretty much whenever I want. I'm James," he said, holding out a hand. "James Gatz."

"Daisy Faye," I said, shaking his hand. His grip was strong and his hand calloused. I was sure I saw motor oil under his fingernails.

"So, you never answered my question," he went on. "What are you doing out here all alone?"

"I wanted some air," I said, then added, "I don't much care for these events. All the patriotic songs. The flag waving. It's all too much for me." His honesty apparently had brought out my own, and I waited for him to lecture me on how much it meant to the boys and how important the war was, and how we were saving the world, but instead he just nodded.

"I imagine they've told you how you keep our morale up and all, you pretty girls." He turned and gave me a quick smile. "Though it is true that looking at a pretty one like you does something for a man's outlook." His grin broadened. "I like your hair."

I shrieked with laughter, then covered my mouth at such an unladylike outburst. His compliment was so sweet and genuine, although it could have been interpreted as more rudeness, as if my hair were my only attractive feature.

"I mean, I like that you haven't cut it like a bunch of the girls have," he went on.

"I'm going to get it cut, though," I said, making the decision then and there. "For the war effort. Don't they need hair for something?"

"I guess they could use it as sort of a decoy, you know, waving it over the edge of a trench so the Germans think there's a pretty fräulein nearby."

"How wonderful—to think of using one's hair to tempt men to run to their deaths. I'll imagine I am Helen of Troy."

"At least they'd die happy thinking they were running to the likes of you," he said, smiling.

"Where are you from?" I asked.

"West of here. Nowhere you would have heard of. It's not where I'm from, though. It's where I'm going. After the war, that is. I'm going to build things, houses and factories and even castles like this one." He swept his arm around toward the country club, and I suppressed a smile that he'd likened the main building to a castle.

"What about you?" he asked. "What are you aiming to do?"

I cocked my head to one side, ready to give the answer all the girls of my age would give. To marry. To bear children. To run a household. But I stopped and instead said, "I want to be loved. Wildly and extravagantly. Absolutely worshipped and never forgotten."

He looked up at me with a bright eagerness, and I knew in that instant he was applying for the job.

We sat and talked there well after the hour my father came by. I saw him sitting in the Ford in the drive at the foot of the steps, reading the newspaper, but Jay—he insisted I call him that even then—continued talking. He didn't talk to me like the other boys who were so eager to make sure you knew how smart and clever they were.

No, Jay asked me about myself. Had I any sisters or brothers? Were my parents alive? Had I lived in Louisville all my life? Did I want to see other places?

No boy who had courted me had wanted to know so much about myself. I didn't even know the answers to many of his questions. They made me think. And by the time I decided to put my father out of his misery and join him in the car, I felt as if Jay were already on the road to adoring me.

"Will you be here next Saturday?" he asked. "It's another dance, but not one of these big war effort shindigs. Just the regular punch and cookies affair."

I smiled. "Yes, yes, I will," I said. "But you might not recognize me. With my bobbed hair."

"Oh, I'd be able to pick you out of a flock of bobbed heads," he said, grinning. "You're the prettiest of them all."

Though I engaged in a dozen other activities the following week, I thought often about that dance. I swam at Lilith's beautiful lake house. On our bright veranda, I painted a picture of bold red geraniums I'd been working on for some time. I took a dancing lesson with Mademoiselle Larchon. And during everything, I thought of what I would wear and whether I should really cut my hair before the event.

Rupert and Andrew and a few other boys came by to call, but they made me feel restless. So I begged off strolls and outings, claiming a headache. Jay didn't come by. He didn't know where I lived, of course, but it bothered me he hadn't tried to find out.

As I brushed my hair the Thursday before the dance and winced at the knots in my unruly tresses, I finally made a decision. I found a pair of scissors and sheared it off, straight across from my chin all the way around the back. Grabbing a mirror, I looked at what I'd wrought. It was shaggy.

"Mother!" I called, hurrying into the hall.

"Oh, my!" she said, her eyes wide as I entered her bedroom. "We should fix that," was all she said. "I'll summon Mrs. Dale."

In a half hour, the woman arrived. She was a tall, stylish brunette who provided fashion advice and arranged coiffures for many in our social set, usually from her small shop downtown.

She passed no judgment on my hair, just worked away, snipping at my rough ends, then shaving my neck. When she was done, I had a cloud of hair around my face that, like Lilith's bob, showed off my features to advantage.

"I'd been wondering when you would want to do this," Mother said.

"She looks very chic," Mrs. Dale said, putting away her implements. "It suits her. She won't have to do a thing to keep it nice, not like some who must curl it or straighten it. Many regret the choice. I had a girl come in—Bernice is her name, from the other side of town—who did it on a dare. She's the plainest girl, so she needed a full long crown of hair to make her something special." She smiled, though she didn't smile often, and patted my shoulder. "You'd look beautiful in any style, my dear."

I saved a lock of my long hair before Mother had the maid clean up the debris, and placed it in a small beaded box on my dresser.

That Saturday, I wore a jewel-red silk with a dropped waist and lace cap sleeves. I sported the lapis lazuli again and adorned my hair with a white diamond clip.

When I walked in the door of the country club, Jay was already waiting there. He had arrived a good hour early, he told me, to make sure he didn't miss me if I decided not to stay long.

"Look at you, all patriotic," he said, taking my hands in his. "Red, white, and blue."

I smiled. "And with bobbed hair."

"Oh, you did something to your hair?" he asked, and I was about to gently hit his shoulder when he laughed and said, "You look mighty fine, like a real princess. I hope you won't mind being escorted by a man who's yet to earn his own noble rank."

It was my turn to laugh. It was just like Jay to act as if one could earn one's way into nobility. "I don't mind at all. I'll just pretend you're already a prince."

I danced every dance with him, and when he wasn't waltzing me around the floor, we wandered outside along the porch and the paths under heavily scented magnolias.

He kissed me for the first time there, under those plump blossoms, and I knew all at once why my other beaux had left me cold. I hadn't fallen in love with them.

That night, I gave him the beaded box with a lock of my hair in it. A few weeks later, in that magnificent red-colored car he'd bragged about, I gave myself to him, becoming Jay Gatsby's lover.

CHAPTER FOUR

The day after meeting Jay at Nick's, a drenching, cleansing down-pour cooled off the earth and sent the Sound into a tempest. It was exhilarating, and part of me wished I had the courage to venture out.

But I didn't. I saw the rain as a directive not to go sailing with Jay, to be careful, which was probably for the best. I didn't even send a note of regret, figuring he'd see the weather and understand.

Still, I could think of little else but him. A calmness descended over me with this glorious secret: I'd found Jay again. Eventually, I pieced together the how and why of it.

Jordan had been to one of Jay's parties, it turned out. He already knew of her connection to me—he had met her once during our Louisville days. She'd told him my cousin lived next door. He had asked her if she could set up a tea for us at Nick's, something for "two old friends who hadn't seen each other in a long time."

But Jordan had known it was more than that. She had seen it in his eyes, in the little trembling in his voice, she said. She had figured out that he'd even moved to West Egg, across from us, precisely so this reunion could eventually come to pass.

So she'd happily talked to Nick about setting up the tea.

Jay occupied all my thoughts after that tea. I had even begged off dinner that night, claiming another headache. In my sitting room alone, I dined on some cold ham and salad, staring out at the water, watching the light bid the day farewell. On my face, a gentle smile appeared, one I couldn't discard.

All these years later. He'd not only remembered me, but longed for me. Even through the war, he had kept a picture of me, he said, in his breast pocket and always looked at it before "going over the top."

Yesterday, he'd pulled out the photograph, an awful thing of me standing rigid and staring at the camera. To this day, he still had it. A tear came to my eye.

Just at a time in my life when I needed to believe in that kind of love, in love at all, he arrived.

He had personally arranged the flowers, the linens, the food, for our little tea. He didn't need to tell me all the details, but he'd extravagantly poured them out. Now I tried hard to remember the precise rose and gold pattern on the cups because it seemed so precious, so tender that he had wanted so earnestly to impress me.

I'd not realized then how assiduously I had been playing a role—that of the sophisticated modern woman— because that's what women did then, after the war, after the plague of the Spanish flu, after death and loss incomprehensible. We all acted on a stage, a comedy with tragic overtones where the jester garners all your sympathy right before his death scene.

I'd been part of that play, trying so hard to grab from the spotlight a sense of life again, of hope, of striving for something better. For meaning.

That's what wanted. Meaning. A reason to be happy and not hurt anymore. I'd not realized how hurt I'd felt, seeing the world I knew disappearing, and seeing the man I married regularly taunting me with words and actions. I covered my pain with a stilted sophistication, as if I was too important to experience sorrow.

I absolutely ached with it, and Jay was like a balm.

Confused, torn between wanting nothing to change and wanting to step into the unknown of this new possibility, I spent the afternoon on the nursery floor, throwing a ball back and forth with Pamela, helping her dress up in my discarded gowns and jewelry, rocking her to sleep for her nap.

Oh, I know I had told Nick I hoped she'd be a little fool, but that was another story meant to startle and then charm, and, as with all stories, it was based on both truth and lies.

The truth was I adored my little girl, and I would do everything in my power to make sure she was no fool, even though I knew the world preferred foolish-seeming women, pliable and empty-headed.

After she was born, Tom had difficulty being with me. My new role as mother must have changed his view of the woman he'd married, and though I regained my svelte figure within several short months, I could tell his attraction to me had waned considerably, and he often had to be drunk to consider lovemaking—with me, that was. He found no such hesitation with other women.

Instead, he treated me either as a fragile goddess he shouldn't provoke or, when liquor peeled off his inhibitions, a woman to punish with a quick and rough bedding.

Although I preferred to keep myself in the former category with Tom, I now wondered, especially after Jordan's urging in this regard, if I could cross the lines that Tom had so easily stepped over, finding warmth and affection elsewhere.

After Pamela's birth, the doctors told me I likely would be unable to bear any more children, so I sometimes wondered if this also accounted for Tom's reticence, knowing he wouldn't be producing any more progeny with me. I dreaded the possibility that he'd foist an unwanted secret son on me some day, born of a mistress I didn't want to know about.

After Pammy fell asleep, the skies calmed, and I pulled on a sweater and walked to the promontory, looking across the Sound to Jay's dock. The boat wasn't there. So he'd gone out despite the rain. With a sigh, I realized I wish I had met him after all. How exciting it would have been for the two of us to battle a storm while sailing his cutter.

Now I'd have to devise a pretext to see him, or hope for an invitation.

I stayed awhile, waiting to see him and his boat return, and at length, I could make out the fine tall shape of his masts and knew he was all right and headed for home. I left before he could see me watching, hurrying around the path and eventually up the walkway to see Tom standing in the door, a note in his hand. I thought he'd been at his club.

"What is it?" I asked, fearing a telegram with bad news.

"Where have you been?" he responded. "Another storm's coming!" He nodded toward the bay, where a thunderhead darkened the horizon.

"I outran it!" I said gaily, unknotting the scarf tied around my hair. "What's that?" I pointed to the envelope in his hand.

"Nothing. An invitation to one of those circuses across the way."

My heart sped up. Jay. I hadn't gone sailing with him, so he'd sent over an invitation. I'd longed for one, and it had appeared, as if by magic.

Tom's attitude, though, seemed to indicate he wasn't about to lower himself to attend.

"Really?" I said, pulling the note from his hands and glancing at the languid script. "What fun! We should go." I tried to sound light, but then I was bold. "Or you can stay here, and I'll report on it for you!"

That tipped him off, and he squinted at me. "I've heard stories of what goes on over there. Not fit for a woman on her own. I'll go, too."

Thus assured of his role as chivalrous protector, he walked back into the house.

The invitation was for two nights from now, and all the next day I chose and discarded dress after dress, wishing I had thought of shopping for something new. And then I realized I did have a new frock, one I'd never worn because Tom had declared it scandalous at dinner with friends in Chicago right before we'd moved.

I found it in the back of my closet and fingered its soft chiffon overlaid with intricate gold embroidery, then quickly donned it.

It *was* scandalous. Pale gauzy chiffon, almost flesh-colored, with a draped neckline that could show hints of real flesh men liked to see. Its embroidery swirled and curved so that it drew attention to breasts and hips before dropping into a cascade of scarf-like layers just below the knees. When I walked, it made me feel like a graceful swan, and I remembered buying it because the gold thread had reminded me of my debutante gown.

I'd had it altered to fit perfectly, thinking Tom would be proud to escort such a unique and tantalizing creature anywhere. Instead, he'd been mildly embarrassed, telling me it made me look as though I wasn't wearing anything at all, and he wasn't going to take a tart to a dinner with important friends.

This time, I would wear no jewelry except a gold bracelet I'd had as a girl, and peacock-colored shoes with tiny heels. Tom would probably object, but I'd tell him I was sure I would look as demure as a nun compared to everyone else at that party.

Nick came by that evening for dinner. The three of us dined on the veranda on vichyssoise, sole meunière, and pommes Lyonnaise, a French meal I'd had Cook prepare to make me think of Jay in France keeping my picture in his pocket everywhere he went. We ate in the blue twilight. When I told Nick we'd received an invitation to a Gatsby party, he nodded.

"They're quite the circus," he said.

"Then maybe we should just go to a circus," Tom said sourly.

"Jordan's gone to one," Nick hastily added, as if this would provide the imprimatur Tom needed. "One of Gatsby's parties. I saw her at one last week. She had a perfectly lovely time, she said."

Last week. Was that when they'd hatched their plan to get me to Nick's cottage to see Jay? I noticed Nick said he'd seen her there, not taken her. As I said, their romance never became a romance, although I knew they'd happily make a couple for any event I chose to hold.

"Two bands, performers, two dinner servings, liquor of every kind," Nick went on, waving his fork as he talked. He seemed excited to share stories of the event to boost Tom's enthusiasm. "So many people, you need to be careful not to accidentally open a door or you might walk in on someone *inamorata*."

Tom leaned back, finished with his meal, and lit a cigarette. "This is supposed to make me want to go?" he asked.

"Oh, Tom, I told you it was all right if you didn't want to. I will be your own personal correspondent and give you a full story on the absurdities of the night. Why, I'm already writing the tale in my head."

"I bet you are," Tom mumbled.

As the maid cleared the plates and brought dessert, the phone rang, and I knew, even before the butler came for Tom, that it would be the Wilson woman. I looked at my husband, smiled, and said sweetly,

"Go on. You know it's for you. I don't mind, as long as you're keeping business humming. I'll just talk to Nick about bonds. Bonds fascinate me, you know. Utterly fascinate me."

Actually, there was some truth to that. I wanted to probe Nick about how one bought stocks and bonds. Jordan was doing it through Nick, and it sounded exciting and useful.

He nodded, looked down, and left, and my smile immediately dropped. Nick and I ate our dessert in silence while Tom's hushed voice traveled onto the veranda. Occasionally a clear word would drift out, and I became embarrassed that we might overhear something that could humiliate me even more than this awkward silence, both Nick and I knowing my husband was on the phone with his lover.

I finished, got up, and went to the balustrade around the veranda, smoking and staring into the shimmering gloaming. Nick joined me.

"Tom's business going well?" he asked.

I laughed. "Oh, stop. We both know he doesn't do any business, and we both know who is on the phone. That Wilson witch." Then I turned to him. "Is she beautiful, Nick? Even in a…a cheap way?"

He grimaced but shook his head. After a pause, he said, looking away from me, "She's not a beauty. She's kind of, well, stout. You have nothing to worry about. Tom loves you. He even roughed her up."

My eyes widened. That Nick had met her was, as I've said, a betrayal. Despite my question, I hadn't expected him to so readily admit it, and for a moment I felt angry that he'd seen her and not immediately insisted they both end their liaisons, or at least come and tell me the whole sordid tale. I also felt betrayed anew by Tom that he had not chosen a beauty, even a cheap one, but instead had settled for someone Nick deemed fat. I didn't think he was lying to me. I think he would have told me the truth. I knew I was pretty. I liked pretty things. I filled our home with them. I thought Tom liked them, too.

"Roughed her up?" I repeated.

Now he did meet my gaze. "Yes. She was saying your name, and Tom didn't want her so much as breathing it. He told her to stop it, but she kept saying it over and over, just to taunt him. Finally, he pulled back and punched her. Well, slapped her is more like it. But it caused an awful ruckus and lots of blood."

Imagining the scene, I bit the inside of my cheek to keep from smiling. Good for Tom, defending his bride. Too bad that defense didn't include fighting off his own bad impulses. I had no illusions about what probably followed his burst of violence.

At least I could be grateful for that, I supposed. Except for the occasional too-tight squeeze, Tom had never laid a finger on me. If he did, I'd leave him for sure.

"Why does he…oh, never mind," I said. I really had no interest in exploring the depths of Tom's melancholia, the reasons he needed to prove over and over what a man he was by building a harem wherever we went. Perhaps I should just let him go on more about the white man's burden. Maybe that would feed his masculine pride.

Nick moved closer and said on a whisper: "You should ask him to stop. I bet he would."

At that, I laughed. Poor, naïve Nick.

"Oh, darling, I'm so glad we've reunited. I need to hear this kind of talk. It reminds me how I used to feel before I became so damned sophisticated."

That was another line I used to charm people, and Nick was appropriately entranced, his eyes shining with sympathy.

This particular line contained more truth than fiction, though. As I moved from girlhood to womanhood, from debutante to wife to mother, I learned the world was cruel, that it injured and killed, that unkindness could be masked by a smile, meanness by good intentions and religious fervor.

We went back to staring out in silence over the darkness, and I became mesmerized by the little green light at the end of our dock, the one Jay told me he looked at, thinking of me.

It shed its glimmer on the ripples of water, and I thought of those ripples making their way across the Sound to him. I wondered at that very moment if he was looking out at that fairy light and seeing me, the true love he had never forgotten. I wanted to measure up to that devotion. I wished I could dive off the promontory and swim to him.

"I think what bothers me most," I said, almost to myself, "is that he can't seem to shake the habit. You know, of seducing women. It seems…dirty in a way that just a long, satisfying affair wouldn't."

"You'd rather he have a lifelong mistress?" Nick asked. I heard the surprise in his voice.

I sighed. "I'd rather he choose…" Me? No, I couldn't say it, not now when I was unsure if it mattered. In fact, it didn't matter. What I wanted wasn't for him to choose. It was for me to choose. With a profound sadness, I realized I wanted to choose to go back, to correct my errors, and marrying Tom seemed like one of them. This was a chasm I couldn't afford to peer into, so I shook those thoughts from my head.

"I'd rather he choose some other scandalous behavior." I laughed. "Perhaps acrobatics or fire juggling or maybe even walking on a tightrope over Niagara Falls! Has anyone done that lately? Maybe we should suggest it!"

Nick laughed softly, then said, "You might see some acrobats at Gatsby's party. Jugglers, too."

"Oh, I hope so. Armies of them! That would be wonderful, if they are very tall and swarthy, with thick black moustaches, and march and juggle at the same time."

"To music, of course!" Nick said, joining in.

"Of course! I can hear it. A snake-charming tune where the dancers have to do complicated steps as they stride through the guests, and we all gasp as they try not to set some poor woman's hair on fire, while we're secretly hoping to see such a disaster."

"You're impossible," Nick said, laughing harder now.

"Am I? Why, thank you, Nick. A high compliment coming from you."

DAISY

As I watched the dock light flicker, I wished I were the most impossible of beings and could be the sparkling green fairy in that lamp, sprinkling magic on everyone around me so I would get what I wanted... after I figured out what that was.

CHAPTER FIVE

T o this day, Nick and I argue about what I wore to that party. He remembers it as a costume event, with a country theme, and describes in detail a peasant outfit I supposedly wore that fit me perfectly and made me the most beautiful woman in the crowd.

I remembered wearing my gauzy gold and cream confection, with the peacock blue slippers and a gold bracelet. Yes, I remembered others in costume, but I didn't mind not having dressed for the occasion. I liked swimming against that tide.

Nick and I disagreed over other details of this whole story, as you know by now. He insists Jay had yet to go to war when I married Tom, but Nick wasn't really in my life at the time and relies on now faulty memories of things. Jay, as you know, was a fabulist, but on that memory we agreed. He left for war, and I married Tom.

Jay himself was in tails and patent leather shoes, and when he saw me, he took in his breath and stammered over his words.

"The Buchanans," he managed to bluster as if a footman making an announcement upon our entering.

No one heard, of course. Not in that meleé.

How to describe it? It *was* a circus, but one you wanted to be a part of, not just observe. It beckoned you to enjoy life, to lift a cup, to sing a song, to dance, to laugh. It felt like a sin not to.

Nick's description had been accurate. There were two bands, one playing all the latest popular tunes. On a big parquet dance platform, couples jounced to the animalistic rhythms of the music. Another band, somewhere upstairs, played waltzes and classical fare for those who couldn't bring themselves to admit they enjoyed savage beats.

There was food and drink everywhere, and people doing outrageous things, wanting to outshine each other. Someone jumped into the pool in full dress just as we came out to that area, and as we made our way to a table, I watched a sopping wet woman, laughing hysterically, being pulled out of the pool by both her arms, one man on each side, her dress dangerously close to sliding down to her waist.

I half expected that army of jugglers I had joked with Nick about to pass by at some point.

Though Tom had ostensibly accompanied me to be my protector, he overcame that impulse quickly enough, along with his snobbish disdain, when he saw two attractive women by a bar and recognized them as moving picture stars. Of course, he had to get something to drink, and it took him nearly an hour to return as he engaged in laughing conversation with them.

I didn't care. The whole thing was an emporium of fun and delight, and, like a patron at a museum, I wandered about drinking in each exhibit, pondering if I liked it or not, passing judgment on the artists who made up the tableau.

Sometimes I walked alone, sometimes with Nick, and often with Jay. Never with Tom.

Presently, Tom appeared at my elbow, holding out a glass of champagne. He polished off his in a gulp, then grimaced. "Not a good vintage, nor a good year."

Buoyed by his pronouncement of personal superiority, he then moved on, deciding to be somewhat generous of spirit. "You do have to hand it to him, though. He might have no taste, but he knows how to make money. There is no way he could pay for all this using borrowed cash. A place like this. Parties every night. Why, he's had palm trees brought up from Florida. See them over there by the pool? No one would do something this extravagant unless he's got capital."

Tom himself would never indulge in such ostentatious displays, but he somehow seemed to envy a man who did. Maybe it was the freedom of it, not caring if others thought you were showing off, but Tom stayed rigidly in his class, his one act of rebellion being his tendency to bed inferior women.

But I knew Jay didn't think of all this as rebellion or ostentatious display. To him, it was simply a boyish sharing of his own happiness, at having achieved what he wanted. His display wasn't a finger in the eye of anyone. It was an outpouring of pure joy.

"He's got a good selection of liquor, too," said Tom. "Talked to him 'bout it. A good deal, he said. Might use his man," Tom added. This after he had just criticized the champagne.

We all moved to a table together and sat down—Nick, me, Tom, and Jordan. Jay was about somewhere, but I didn't see him as Tom babbled on about investments, deals on liquor, and more.

In recent months, Tom had been talking more and more about "deals." He seemed to think he was missing out, just letting his fortune accumulate the old-fashioned way, and he'd become interested in investing, growing his capital. Talking to his father about it, too. I let him go on. It was a better way of feeding his manhood than accumulating mistresses. Or pummeling them. And I picked up information from these brief conversations, especially when Nick was around to offer advice.

"Gatsby was telling me about buying stocks on margin," Tom now announced. "Nick, you learn anything about that in all your midnight-oil burning at the Yale Club library?"

Nick reddened. "If you have the money, sure, buying on margin is a good way to accumulate a lot of stock quickly. It holds some risk…"

Tom clapped him on the shoulder. "Risk for those without money. Maybe I'll talk to you about this some time. I have an idea we're all going to need to fortify our homes, take care of ourselves, as the lower races attempt their ascent to the top."

Before he could go on, a short, balding man in a constable costume nearly tipped over our table as he clumsily tripped and fell into it.

"Say, watch it," Tom said, now rising to his protector role.

Jay caught sight of the problem, and rushed over, putting his arm around the fellow.

"Steady there, old sport." To us, he said, "This is Anthony Delacorte," as if we should know who that was. "Big into imports, exports," he added when he noticed our blank stares.

Anthony took that as an invitation to join us and promptly sat down in the only empty chair at the table. Jay beamed at me with raised eyebrows, standing behind Anthony.

I closed my eyes and gave my head the tiniest of shakes, trying to convey that I couldn't get away from Tom right there.

"Jay here's a great man, y'know. Not just a great frien'. He's got good music, books." Delacorte waved his arm, almost smacking a passing woman in an elaborate peasant frock who didn't seem to notice. "Went to Oggsfur, y'know."

"Oggsfur?" I asked. "What's that?"

Jay looked down and suddenly left us, walking with a sense of taking over the band, as if he had to alert them to some special request.

"It's in London. Or round there," Mr. Delacorte informed us, shouting over the noise. "You haven't heard of it? Most famous college in the world, by golly." He looked at me with suspicion, as if I were teasing him.

"Oh, Oxford," I said, finally understanding. "But Jay couldn't possibly have gone to Oxford." Not if he was making his fortune. Why would he waste time on college, even one like "Oggsfur"?

"Seen a pitt-chur of him there with some of his buddies," the man said. "Go on, ask him. He went to Oggsfur'."

I sighed and looked for Jay in the teeming swirl of humanity. He had disappeared. I had no doubt he'd spun that tale to friends, acquaintances, and business associates, and it saddened me while also igniting a fire of sympathy, a desire to defend him. In that story, he had been trying to impress, or at least fit in with the Toms of the world. Why do that, Jay? You don't need to.

He shouldn't feel the need to try to impress these people, especially people like Tom. Tom had gone to Yale, but I had met enough of his fellow alumni to suspect that their education had been more about making the right kind of friends than the actual pursuit of wisdom or any kind of meaning.

Tom wasn't even listening by now, his gaze scanning the crowd for more suitable people to talk with. Soon, he went to the bar for a refill, and it wasn't long before he was deep in conversation with a pale-skinned redhead in a dress of the same hues as mine.

Anthony Delacorte left our table, too, and Jay returned. This seemed to be a signal for Jordan and Nick to go, as well. They sprang up as Jay sat down, so the two of us were alone in that swirling throng of partyers. There were so many of them, making so much noise with laughter and talking and even singing that it felt as if we were alone. Jay placed his hand over mine and looked into my eyes.

"I've missed you," he said.

"It has been several years," I answered.

"No. I mean since the other day. At Nick's. I've missed you since then. I've counted every second."

"I've missed you, too." This was no lie, and I felt so comfortable here with him that it became even more apparent to me how much I pretended in front of Tom and others. With Jay, I felt relaxed. I became who I really was, even if I didn't quite know who that was.

"Daisy, come over any time you want. Any time. I'll always be waiting for you. Always." He pulled my hand to his lips and kissed it.

There is nothing more intimate than two people in a noisy crowd. We existed in a place all our own, as if we were invisible to the throng around us, as if we were king and queen of this fairyland, and our subjects were cavorting secretly for our pleasure. If Jay had made love to me right there in that moment, I would have believed no one could see us.

Hours later, when Jay was interrupted by a servant asking a liquor supply question, the spell was broken. Nonplussed, Jay grabbed me by the elbow, looked around, and whispered, "Let's go!" He nodded toward Nick's place.

Did I know that, by accepting this invitation, I was crossing a line? Yes, even if I didn't articulate it to my conscience. I burned for Jay. I remembered how he had touched me when we were young. He was my first lover. I'd been no perfect flower on my wedding night.

"Nick!" I cried, spotting him as we meandered toward the front door. "We're going to sit on your steps and talk. Will you mind, darling, sounding the alarm if Tom comes looking for me, though I doubt that'll be any time soon?" I moved to see Tom dancing with one of the moving picture stars now.

"Sure thing."

"Thanks, old sport," Jay said to Nick, and as soon as we were out of the light and into the shadows, he grabbed my hand and we raced like children down the little hill and through the small stand of trees that separated his property from Nick's rented place.

Giggling and breathless, we neared Nick's steps, and I knew, as Jay pulled me into an embrace and a long, deep kiss, that we wouldn't be doing much talking here.

This, I realized was the moment when I discarded the last of my girlish rules. I knew it as soon as we stepped onto Nick's porch and opened his door. There on the threshold, my mind was whispering yes over and over to my heart, and I felt no remorse, no guilt, not even a pinch of indecision.

Jay pulled me into an embrace at the door, and when he felt me respond with equal fervor, he began to kiss my neck, my shoulders, and my hands. I remember—oh, God, I remembered—what it was like to be adored so, to be cherished and treated as something fine and beautiful.

I felt fine and beautiful, the moonlight glinting off the gold thread on my shimmering fairy dress.

Jay lifted me into his arms and took me to the guest bedroom, where, in our eagerness, we stripped each other until we were in the bed. Here was a lover who made me feel as if I was the only woman on earth he could ever have.

Whether inspired by drink, Jordan's talk, or my own musings on fidelity, I no longer had any doubts. I had tolerated Tom's wandering. Now he'd have to tolerate mine. But unlike him, I wouldn't flaunt it, and at least my choice was our equal in wealth if not in status.

From across the way, we heard the muted sounds of the party, music from the pool area and the upstairs salon creating discordant melodies, a pure line of Mozart on strings interrupted by the slide of a trumpet pulsating up the scale to some victorious wail of ecstasy. We heard laughter and the occasional crash, perhaps of a tray or glass. We heard a woman yelling, as clearly as if she were next to us, "Just shut up about it!" And I thought I picked up the splash of the pool—perhaps another woman had imitated the first.

It felt like the best place on earth. In Nick's guest room that night. Just on the very edge of frivolity, it was close enough to enjoy without having to witness its distasteful details, letting its waves lap at our feet, not drowning in its depths. This was what I'd craved, a sweet sample of exuberant life, at a distance, to keep me safe.

I wanted to stay there forever, close to home, yet far enough way, close to those I loved—Pamela, and, yes, Jay—and not cut off from the hubbub of life that could make it so much fun.

DAISY

After our passion had exhausted itself, he asked softly, "Why didn't you wait for me?"

I was stroking his cheek as he tried to balance on his elbows so as not to crush me with his weight. He was still finely muscular, like a statue of a Greek god. I wondered if he boxed or lifted barbells. I reached up and touched a firm shoulder.

"Oh, Jay," I said. "I thought…I didn't think you'd…"

"Make it home?" he answered and sat up, grabbing and holding my hand, bringing it to his lips again.

His gestures were gentle, not angry, just like his tone, so I nodded in the dim light.

"I was so afraid then. Of so many things."

"Aw, Daisy, you had to know you'd see me again. I would have done anything to get back to you. We all had gals we wanted to return to."

"Not everyone returned," I said.

"You didn't get my letters," he said.

I paused. His letters. I'd received one the night before my wedding to Tom. I didn't want to tell Jay I had read it. That seemed too cruel to both of us, after we'd just found each other again. I wanted to be the woman who *would* have stopped her wedding after reading such a letter, and I didn't want him to know I wasn't.

"On the eve of my wedding to Tom," I said on a breath. "One— just one—arrived then. The night before." This was sufficiently vague, I decided, not suggesting I'd read it, only that I had received it.

He leaned back, taking this in, and then pulled me to him. I rested my head on his strong shoulder, and we didn't speak. He kissed me on the head, just as Edouard had done to his wife at the speakeasy, and this, too, felt right, part of the balancing of my world.

I don't know what Jay was thinking, but he seemed to accept my statement as a suitable explanation, even if he had preferred another outcome. At last, he said, "But you never loved him."

So that was the calculation he had been making, the conclusion he'd been finding his way to. Sweet man, he needed to hear I loved him alone. Had he been equally faithful, I wondered? Surely not. Why did men think they had the right to claim uninterrupted devotion from women they would forget in an instant whenever they themselves found a charming substitute? But Jay hadn't forgotten me, I reminded myself. He had built a life around not forgetting me.

"Oh, Jay, I was numb." The night before my wedding and the day of, I was someone else observing all that was happening, a smile on my face, little sparks of joy flashing from time to time, but nothing that started a fire like this one—the one we'd just enjoyed. I'd been a different person then, and I didn't want to talk about that girl with Jay. There was only this Daisy in this moment.

He hugged me tight and kissed the top of my head again, satisfied.

We lay there for quite some time until I heard footsteps rustling through the brush on the border of Jay's property, so we promptly dressed and walked to the front steps, holding hands. We sat down and Jay lit a cigarette for me.

DAISY

When Nick approached, it looked as if we had been there, just talking, for the past hour.

"Tom's looking for you," Nick said. I saw his eyes gleam in the light spilling from Jay's mansion. "Wants to go home. Sent the chauffeur, who's out front."

I stood, and Jay handed me my wrap, which had fallen onto the steps behind me, gently pressing it around my shoulders. He placed a bold kiss on my cheek, and I leaned into him for a last embrace.

Together, we headed back to Jay's mansion, where Nick and I found Tom and Jordan in the main hall. Jay followed shortly after, as if he'd been somewhere else on the property. Soon we were all scurrying to the car, hastening inside, the cool night air erasing any dark moments from before.

"Don't hesitate to come back anytime!" Jay called to us, but I knew he was speaking only to me.

As we pulled away, I reached out the window to wave. I knew Jay would be standing on the steps watching.

CHAPTER SIX

I did go back. In fact, I went back the very next afternoon. Tom woke up that day hung over, and once recovered from his over-imbibing, drove into the city again, maybe to pursue some of those new deals he was enthused about and maybe to see Myrtle. Likely both.

I didn't care. I really didn't. Not a wisp of vexation blew into my blue-sky happiness. Feeling light and wholesome, I hopped into our Ford and made my way over to Jay's, as if this was the life I was meant to lead, going to a lover who had spent years trying to woo me, even if I'd been unaware of it. We were mending a cloth ripped open by war, stitching it together again, thread by thread, so this, too, felt like something greater than ourselves—greater, even than our own personal happiness.

Despite my joy, there was at first a strange awkwardness to our meeting that afternoon. The maid ushered me in, telling me to wait in a small parlor off the front door. I wasn't convinced she would really fetch Jay, and I walked around the room looking at the *objets d'art* on various shelves, deciding to call out his name if he didn't appear soon and then head home. Was that a Fabergé egg, a Japanese porcelain plate, a Meissen figurine?

In the corner was a plain wooden desk, the kind a schoolboy might use. Bending over it, I saw his initials carved in the corner, barely visible: JG. My hand floated over it, this remnant of a past of which I knew little.

When Jay had entered my life in Louisville, he had no past. He was one of many soldiers billeted nearby, and their uniforms created class equality. Rich and poor were identical. When he came to that dance at the local club, I was blissfully unaware of his social class. I only knew he was smart and kind and honest.

It seems strange to contemplate now how I almost missed this meeting. My feelings about the war had been part personal spite and part prescient foreboding. I thought it all silly and awful and wasteful. To voice those opinions was heresy.

But my mother knew how to gently push me into doing the right thing, whether I had the spirit for it or not, and maybe it really hadn't been so hard for her to nudge me into attendance. I liked parties at the country club. I liked being on my own, seeing who I could flirt with, charm, entrance. I'd felt pretty that night, contrarily so, with my unbobbed hair and lack of much jewelry, with little decoration on my dress, and a scant bit of powder on my face, just enough to keep perspiration from making it shine.

My contrarian mood dimmed my spirits a bit as I tried to decide whether to give in to my inclination to have a good time or hold tight to my resentment at being forced to pretend support for a cause I didn't believe in. Why were men always so eager to show they could kill and die?

Looking back, I see how that contrarianism served me well. It kept me out on the porch, ready for the moment when Jay arrived that night. If I had been inside, dancing, laughing, talking with friends, would he have noticed me or only seen me as one of the crowd of pretty girls?

And my contrary nature had kept me faithful to Tom all these years, even when I'd been tempted—by Edouard and a few others—to stray. No, not faithful to Tom, I decided. Faithful to the idea of the kind of love I'd shared with Jay. Now I had it again.

"Daisy!" Jay walked into the room, heading toward me with long strides. He kissed me immediately, holding my arms and looking at me, as if years had not parted us, as if it were the day after that country club dance, and our future together was settled. "You came!"

"You invited me," I reminded him.

"Yes, yes," he said and put his arm around me, guiding me toward a big sunroom at the back of the house. "I'm so glad you came."

He seemed distracted, though. He looked over my shoulder. Was he expecting someone else?

"This is a bad time for you," I suggested. I didn't want to be humiliated, and I began to feel that once again I had dreamed up an affection that wasn't as deep as I'd first imagined. I was new to this, after all, crossing the line Tom had a habit of hopping over.

"No, not at all," he said as he closed a door to the sunroom behind us. "I just…I don't want staff gossiping. I want you safe." He reopened the door. "I will be right back."

Then I heard him in the hallway telling a servant that everyone was off for the day, with pay. The maid, or whoever it was, protested she had a lot of work left to do, but Jay insisted they all be gone within the quarter hour.

"There," he said, returning. He sat next to me on a cushioned settee. "We're all alone."

And we were. With a thrill, I realized the entire house was now our playroom, and it didn't take us long to make good use of it. No hurried lovemaking on a guest room bed this time. He took my hand and led me slowly to his own bedroom, picked me up, carried me over its threshold, then laid me on crisp laundered sheets and told me he had never stopped loving me. And never would. Our lovemaking was slow and sensual, different from our first hurried sessions when we were young and had to steal moments in discreet places. These were different from Tom's awkward beddings, where I sometimes felt the need to reassure him that he was doing all right.

This coming together was a dance of pure bliss, both of us enjoying each other, with nothing to prove.

We swam in his pool, too, naked and unashamed, and made love like sea creatures finding each other in the depths.

It was the first of many contented afternoons spent together. We danced, we talked, we laughed, we swam, we made love.

Oh, to be forever young! That's how I felt on those serene days. Worries faded, even the future disappeared. Just those moments of joy remained, and it was like revisiting the past, those lovely days of feeling loved unconditionally by the world. Yet my pleasure was now a hundredfold amplified because I now knew just how rare it was to feel this way.

Jay's parties ceased. Once he and I became lovers, he didn't want the house full of strangers, no matter how star-studded the guest list might be. He told me he had sometimes found a stray guest in his home mornings after parties. He wouldn't risk that.

That changed with us. So careful was he with my reputation, that he even changed his staff, hiring men and women Mr. Delacorte recommended to him, who knew, he told me, that their jobs and their lives depended on their discretion.

There would be no town gossip about us, and I was able to drive myself over to Jay's place in the afternoons, often when Tom went riding or into town to make the many deals he now seemed to be fascinated with. I suspected Jay had something to do with those deals, enticing him into one meeting or another with men of finance and industry. Tom would have loved mingling with that crowd, feeling as if he were an agent of business and not an idler whose best years had faded behind him.

Tom had even started using Jay's liquor supplier—an arrangement I wasn't particularly fond of because I feared the bootlegger wouldn't be as discreet as Jay's home staff. So I made a point several nights in a row of reminding him how he'd criticized Jay's champagne, complained of the taste of the gin, and groaned about the sourness of the wine, intimating it must have been cheap liquor labeled to look like top-shelf brands. I suggested to Tom that he might have been taken in by unscrupulous providers who knew he had the cash to throw around. That was enough for Tom. He stopped ordering, even stiffed the supplier on a bill for the last delivery, telling him he wouldn't pay for goods that weren't real. He didn't stop his forays into business, though.

That left Jay and me in the clear, and the summer began in earnest as an idyll drenched in love. I felt as bright as the flickering fairy in the light at the end of our dock. I felt that my line about the longest day of the year being worth remembering, yet often forgotten, was true. The burst of light on that day was a beacon for the rest of the summer. For life itself.

It's odd to think back now and realize that that summer was just a single summer, because it felt at the time as if it lasted a year, a decade, an eon, while the rest of the world raced forward without us.

I was lucky our first few weeks. Tom was often gone when I returned home, and, even when home, disinterested in where I'd been. I always had an excuse at the ready—I'd gone into town to look at clothes for Pamela, I'd taken a drive, I'd played golf with Jordan. I had a veritable book of excuses all ready to offer.

Sometimes, on those languorous afternoons, we would sit in his parlor listening to records—beautiful French music, new tunes, Broadway melodies, jazz groups. He'd silently get up to change the record, then come back to repose by my side, giving me a glance of understanding, intimating a strange kind of ennui that was part regret, part hopefulness.

For hours we'd lounge there, smoking and listening, not saying a word, just caressing each other's arms when something particularly sweet would float into the room, immediately communicating that we understood the mood of the musical artist. It was a game, to wordlessly go long periods, to feel utterly understood in the slightest movement, tilt of the head, blink of the eye.

Sometimes, he took me on drives in his ostentatious car, on back roads so no one would see us, even though I enjoyed wearing dark glasses and hideous scarves, cultivating stories of who I was playing that day—a Russian spy, a deposed aristocrat, or a shopkeeper's daughter on a lark. I joked that I might start wearing wigs of different colors.

"Your reputation will be ruined, Jay, but mine will be intact," I said.

To which he replied, "No man's reputation is ruined by being with a beautiful woman."

Some days we went sailing, though I worried during those outings that someone from my house would spot us from our house. Jay always got us quickly out of the Sound, though, and we would sail until our houses disappeared from view, anchor in some quiet cove, and make love in the gently rocking cabin, the boat moving in time with our passion. We were the only beings alive.

It all passed as if a dream, and I felt, for the first time in years, young and hopeful, even if I wasn't sure what I was hoping for. It was how I felt as a girl, that the future held even more happiness, and each day would be like unwrapping a beautiful present selected just for me.

Jay shared that optimism. That's why I'd fallen for him. He had not gone on to build all those things he'd wanted to build, he told me one afternoon, but he'd built other things. Business connections, deals. I knew he dealt in bootlegged liquor, but in those days, that was no sin. If anything, it was virtue of a contrarian sort, the kind I understood well. He had also made considerable investments in stock, he said. I asked him to teach me how to invest, and soon I'd set up my own account through Nick—so I could get in on the party.

If I was careful to have at-the-ready excuses for my afternoon absences, I was careless with my mood. Although I started the summer melancholic and slow, I couldn't keep a smile off my face now, and I practically danced through the house with Pamela whenever we played together.

Tom commented on my change in mood one afternoon after I'd been giggling so hard with Pamela that I collapsed in tears after running races with her in the hall.

Tom stood and stared with narrowed eyes as I laughed uncontrollably on the floor.

"You've changed," he said, and it wasn't clear he thought it was for good or ill.

"I'm…I'm happy here," I offered, and as soon as the words came out of my mouth, I worried I had misspoken. Tom seemed to yank things away from me if he knew I liked them. Though I had not fallen in love with Chicago, I hadn't liked the idea of moving, unless it was back to Louisville. The more I'd argued for a Kentucky destination, the more committed he'd become to our relocation in New York. He had said it was for business, but Tom did no real business that I could see at that point of our lives. He enjoyed pretending he had his finger in this or that, just so he didn't feel left out. That's why Gatsby's connections excited him so. He finally did get to be around the rulers of Wall Street, of commerce, and they treated him like an equal.

When we moved here, I'd heard the rumors. He had gotten us out of Chicago because of a mistress whose brother was a mobster or something comparable. I couldn't keep all of his infidelities straight. Perhaps he thought prolonged absence and physical distance would tamp down her ire at his refusal to leave me for her.

I wondered sometimes how strongly he would feel about that over the years—not leaving me.

"Well, you've worked up poor Pammy," he said, pointing to our daughter, who was out of my arms and jumping up and down for more foot races. "Where's Nanny?"

I stood, dropped my smile, and called for our daughter's minder, who came round the corner and grabbed Pamela by the hand, leading her to the nursery for her afternoon snack.

"You've worked yourself up, too," he said, and I pushed an errant lock from my eyes. "You look feverish. Are you sure you're all right?"

I was more than all right. I was gloriously, exuberantly happy. But obviously, those moods were not permitted in our household, at least not for me.

"I'm perfectly fine, dear. But you look a little peaked," I said, walking toward the stairs.

"Maybe we should have Dr. Prinz come look in on you." he called after me, with narrowed eyes.

So now I knew that Tom preferred me unhappy, or at least melancholic, and I would have to cover my gladness if I didn't want to arouse suspicions. So I began pretending horrible headaches or other odd ailments from time to time. I also set up luncheons with family—Nick—and friends—Jordan and some of her golfing colleagues—where I could loll about as if everything was a bother and I was bored with all the world had to offer. I even talked of taking a cure somewhere, maybe in Europe.

That thought intrigued me. I longed to get away, to leave behind pretense and bask in a happiness I didn't have to hide.

My life became what I'd imagined it would be long ago, filled with happiness and pleasure. Mornings I spent with wifely and motherly tasks. I planned meals with Cook, chose linens, picked place settings. Then I'd spend time with dear Pamela, taking her for walks when Nanny was occupied, reading to her, even teaching her to play some basic notes on the piano. Occasionally, I went on shopping sprees, buying her new clothes, even some jewelry, and treating myself to a new treasure along the way.

And the afternoons were just for me, golden times for a golden girl, sailing, lounging, making love with Jay, worshiped by Jay, adored by Jay.

For once, I was glad Tom had other temptations in his life and often went into the city, or went riding, or otherwise occupied himself. I didn't know if he was still seeing the Wilson woman or some other wench. At that point, I cared so little about him that I didn't even bother to ask Nick.

Nick and Jordan were the only two who knew of my affair with Jay, and though I sensed that Nick didn't approve, he never said anything to me about it other than to comment that Gatsby's new staff didn't seem to keep the lawns as well manicured as before. Jordan, I knew, approved.

What you have to understand about Nick is that he could be something of a prude. In his telling of our story, I'm a sexless nymph, and you're lucky if you can conjure up a flesh and blood image of me. I'm an alien creature whose daughter sprang fully formed from my rib at age three, I supposed.

But back then, it would have been shocking to say too much about the intimacies of married life, of lovers' lives. So I can understand how in that first iteration of the tale, Nick pulled the curtain on details most audiences weren't prepared to see.

So I will correct some of those omissions with this: Jay was a wonderful lover, gentle and eager and never going beyond what he sensed I wanted to do, yet still a manly partner with no inhibitions about his own pleasure.

I knew I was living in a dream, a paradise whose snake could soon offer someone an apple too appealing not to eat, tossing us all out into a cold and judgmental universe. I forcefully pushed that knowledge from my mind. I willed the summer to last forever. I willed Tom to leave me alone. I willed Jay to keep loving me.

Finally, as August approached, both the men in my life pulled me from the heights back to the ground, and as I floated down to my perch, I had to decide: Do I stay with Tom, or do I leave with Jay?

CHAPTER SEVEN

Jordan sat across from me at L'Aiglon on Fifty-Fifth Street, puffing on a cigarette as she perused the menu. I had set up this luncheon, suggesting we go shopping in the morning, then have a nice meal. We'd spent an enjoyable hour wandering Fifth Avenue shops but saw nothing except some new hats that suited our fancy. Those were to be delivered the next day, and I felt a sense of accomplishment for finding something to buy when the purpose of this meeting wasn't to acquire things but to seek advice on discarding men. Or at least one man.

We placed our orders for lamb chops and asparagus with Hollandaise sauce, then Jordan sat back, peered at me, and breathed out a plume of smoke.

"Speak," she said, and I smiled.

"I want to leave Tom," I said.

At that, she nodded, and her lack of surprise buoyed me. "Jay wants to move to Europe. He thinks we'll feel more free there."

Again, she nodded, but this time it annoyed me because it felt as if she had known I should do this all along but hadn't bothered to let me in on her secret plan for me. I paused, and she finally spoke. "You don't want to go?"

"Oh, yes, I do. I would love to go. The problem is, Tom wants to go, too."

At that, she chuckled, then stubbed out her cigarette as she leaned into the table. "With you and Jay, I assume."

I giggled and gave a fake shudder. "No, thank God. One man is enough." Then I frowned, realizing my problem. One man *was* enough, and, at the moment, I had two.

"So Tom wants to go to Europe—another Tour? Didn't you just get back from one?" she pressed.

I nodded. "Last year. It was lovely. I think Tom felt cheated, though, with everything still being a bit awful after the war. He says things are better now, more cleaned up."

Jordan smirked. "How clever of those French to tidy everything up for him."

I ignored her sarcasm. "I'd love to go. To get away. I wasn't really keen on moving East, you know. Tom had told me we'd move back to Louisville at some point, and then he bought the house in East Egg without even telling me." I didn't go on about the reasons. I was sure Jordan already knew the sordid tale of the mobster's sister. Tom seemed to like playing in that world, and I wondered if the risk of it thrilled him. Maybe he'd mistaken Myrtle for a gangster's moll, and that's what had attracted him to her.

"You never seemed like a New York girl to me," she said, "but I love the city. I might get a permanent place here."

"Oh, but I do love New York. I think I'd prefer being in the city. Sometimes I feel so cut off from everything. Tom didn't consult me before we moved here, and I thought, if we did move, it would be back home."

"Home," she repeated, her mouth twitching up at the corner. I wondered if she considered any place home. "Do go on, though," she continued. "About wanting to get away."

"From Tom," I amended.

"You do that already, though, don't you? Get away from Tom? I thought you were enjoying all that mightily. He's not on to you, is he?"

For Jordan, it was as simple as that. I had a good thing going. Keep it going. If she saw nothing wrong in what Tom did, she would not judge me, either.

I chewed at my lip, wondering if I was the one in the wrong. I wanted only one man, and I didn't want to have him only on the sly.

"I don't want to keep doing this," I said softly. "I'm not like Tom. I can't keep...pretending."

"Are you pretending, though? You have a perfectly sweet life with Tom and Pamela, and an equally exquisite one with Jay. There's no pretense in that, dear."

I frowned. Sometimes Jordan's frankness could be maddening. "I can't be like Tom," I repeated. "I won't."

She accepted that, even if she didn't agree with my rationale. "So you need to choose between them? If that's it, let's draw up some cards, score each man according to value and skills. Where shall we start?" Her voice gained enthusiasm as she talked, and she pulled up her handbag and withdrew from it an old golf card, on the back of which she began to write with a stub of a pencil. "Amorous abilities?" she suggested with a mischievousness lopsided grin.

I smiled. "Oh, Jordan, you are exactly what I need right now. It's a serious problem, but it weighs me down. I need to be lifted up."

"You need a cocktail, and so do I, but that will have to wait." She leaned in again. "Let's do get serious, though. I have no preferences on who you should be with. I see both men's flaws and both men's virtues. Or rather, their values. Tom is good-looking, from a great family, has money. Jay is good-looking, a man of the times, has money. They both love you—"

"Tom?" I interrupted with a cynical laugh.

"You equate fidelity with love. He doesn't. Now, close your eyes and tell me, who do you see yourself with, years from now? Old and withered, gray hair, sagging skin, raspy voice?"

I did as she said, closing my eyes with a smile on my face. "Do I need to sway? Perhaps chant something? Is this like a séance?"

"Yes. But don't be too loud. We are in a public place, and I'm quite hungry and would like to eat before we're kicked out."

Still smiling, I said, "Okay. I see myself with…Jay. No, Tom. No, Jay. No…" I sighed, opened my eyes, and said, "Pamela."

"There's a story," she said. "Tell it." But then our meals arrived. We both paused as the steaming plates were set in front of us.

"Jay never asks about her," I said. "I sometimes think he forgets I have a daughter. He's so eager to have us be who we were years ago, before my marriage, before Pamela."

"Do you talk about her?" she asked after taking a bite of lamb.

"Rarely. I guess I don't because he seems so disinterested, and I don't want to spoil the mood."

"So you don't think his European plan includes her? Is that what you're saying?" She took a drink of water and I took the time to eat, though my appetite wasn't keen.

Avoiding a direct answer, I went on, "Tom, on the other hand, would probably fight tooth and nail to keep her. Not because she means as much to him—though I know he adores her—but because it would be a way of punishing me."

Jordan frowned, dabbing at her mouth with a napkin. "Tom, he's never physically hurt you, has he?"

"Oh, no, no!" I said. "I did hear the most delicious story of him hitting that Wilson witch, though. I have to admit it made me happy. Felt like I was the one throwing the punch."

She put down her fork and stretched her tan arm toward mine, placing her hand on my wrist. "Listen to you," she said seriously. "You like the idea of smacking around his mistress. Is it because you still love him?"

Now it was my turn to frown. "No! I mean, not enough. I just don't like him betraying me."

"You are kind of doing the same thing, though. I'm not judging you, just pointing out the truth. I think it's fine you've been seeing Jay. You're happy again."

"But Tom..." *Started it*, I'd been about to say, to justify my own infidelity. I pushed at the food on my plate, sighed again, and sat back. "I don't know what to do. This summer, it's been like magic. It's re-awakened me. I feel part of life again. I want things. I hope for things. I'm ready to...to change."

Jordan cocked her head to one side, holding her fork in midair. "How so?"

"I just know I'm tired of things the way they are, and I'm not going to keep living a life I don't much like." It had been the life I'd aspired to, but as I looked back to my pre-marital days, I realized now that I'd made false assumptions. I assumed that life would take on more meaning once I was married, and then, once I had a child, an even deeper meaning. I married and had a child, and yet meaning remained elusive, and while that wouldn't have bothered me so much just a couple years ago, it began to erode any happiness I did happen to experience. It colored everything. It raised questions: So what? To what end?

"That sounds rather drastic, dear, talking of melancholy when you're something of a pampered princess." She ate for a few moments, then said, "I apologize. I shouldn't make light of it. I know you've been unhappy. Tom can be an absolute boor at times, and Gatsby—well, I think there are a thousand women who'd swoon at the possibility of being the object of his attention. So I do understand, really. I suppose what might help is if you start thinking of technicalities. Not being on the eighteenth hole but plotting how you get to the eighteenth hole, shot by shot."

"Is that what you do?" I asked her.

"Yes. Until I reach the point where a little slip of my toe might help nudge things in the right direction." She smirked again. Jordan had been accused of cheating on the links, but it had never been proven. To that day, I didn't know if she was innocent or not. If guilty, she probably didn't think of it as cheating but just another way to play the game. Then again, she might have enjoyed the thought that some people assumed she had cheated even if she hadn't. It made them fear her.

Nevertheless, Jordan was right. It was time to stop dreaming and start planning. And the first hole would have to be Jay's acceptance of Pamela. I would have to risk spoiling the mood to rid myself of anxiety. It would take courage, something I was beginning to realize I had little of. It had been the reason I'd married Tom. The reason I stayed with him. The reason I hated thinking of sacrificing a scintilla of happiness by forcing Jay to accept me as a mother of a beautiful girl, not just as a lover.

We finished our meals and went to the car: Tom's little coupe, which he'd let me take for our excursion into the city. It had been glorious fun driving it. I was a good driver, just as I was a good sailor.

As I pushed the car into gear and began our journey home, Jordan asked, "Do you still have it? The letter?"

DAISY

I knew what she was talking about, the crumpled bit of paper Jay had sent me and I received on the eve of my wedding. The one he'd asked about the night we'd made love, at Nick's house when I'd pretended I'd gotten it but not read it.

"Yes," I said, my eyes on the road ahead.

INTERLUDE
1918

On the day Jay shipped out, I was sure I'd see him again. His own self-confidence seemed to block out all doubt and fear. He had been to our house for dinner several times before then, and both my parents took to him, though Mother more than Father. She liked his cheerful ambition, she said. It reminded her of her grandfather, who, unlike my father, who'd inherited money, had made his fortune by owning and buying several stores, and had always been keen on the future, even during troubled times, she told me.

Jay talked about his plans after the war, and he sounded ever more optimistic—he would own a railroad company or maybe an oil field or perhaps a car manufacturer since he knew a good deal about the process.

He seemed so sure of himself that you found yourself focusing on his post-war ideas instead of the battles he faced, as well as accepting as fact that he would return unscathed.

When we said our final farewells the night before he was to leave, he wouldn't let me get teary. He lifted my chin up and said, "I'll write you every week, every day, and I'll keep your picture and lock of hair in my pocket. Don't you worry, Daisy. I'll stay true to my word."

But no letter came a week later, or two weeks after that, or even a month beyond his departure.

DAISY

I ran to the mailbox every day to see what was in it. I received letters from Rupert and Andrew, but nothing from Jay. I wrote him. At least at the beginning.

Lilith heard from her fiancé, and Candace from hers, and then came the devastating news that Helen Beaufort's Theodore died in combat. Shortly after that, word arrived that Dewitt had been grievously injured and might never see again.

The world turned black. I walked to the mailbox timidly, slowly, expecting to receive a letter with bad news from one of Jay's friends. Either that, or I had to face the fact that he had lied to me and didn't love me at all, that his battle duty was an escape from entanglement with me. Both scenarios covered my days with grim dreariness.

You would think from Nick's recounting of our story that we didn't face heartache except of our own making, that we didn't face dramatic losses and awful events that took lives and futures. In his account, he ignored the war years, maybe intentionally, because he, like some men, didn't like to talk about them. Once U.S. involvement produced an armistice, so many wanted just to forget and move on, embracing a wild hedonism to scour out the wounds.

But the war colored everything that happened afterward, in personal lives or general history. The war and the sickness that overlapped its ending had us all reeling. It seemed so pointless, all that suffering. What was gained? If I'd been cynical before about the patriotic fervor that sent men into the mauling war machine, I was even more jaded after. Nothing seemed to matter.

Every day crawled by. Yet every sunrise I wished the days would last longer so that I might receive news—some news, any news.

I worried the army wouldn't know to contact me about Jay, or where. We weren't formally engaged though he'd talked of marriage and it had been understood we'd be together when he returned. He'd given me a small ring, something simple that had belonged to his grandmother, he said, a thin gold band with a tiny pearl. It was too big, so I wore it on a chain around my neck.

I stopped going to dances. I made myself sick with worry. I wrote letters to the army to ask about him, but then tore them up before mailing, disgusted with my pathetic pleading.

Staying away from social events seemed the patriotic thing to do now, so I could hide my sadness behind a mask of responsibility.

My father became distracted by all of it, and retreated to his study early every evening, sometimes even eating dinner alone there, his mood glum.

This went on for months as 1917 dragged into the new year until Mother stood in my bedroom door and ordered me to stop moping.

"You can't do a thing about him," she announced, "and Jeanine March is hosting a party this weekend for her daughter, who's marrying next month. We'll all go. You know her—Claire."

So we went. It was such an unusually cold night that I simply couldn't get warm even though I wore a dark blue long-sleeved serge dress and draped a Russian shawl over my shoulders.

DAISY

The Marches owned a huge house—much larger than ours—on the outskirts of town. Mrs. March had rearranged their very large parlor for dancing, with furniture pushed up against the walls, and a table set up with refreshments. Claire had forgone a coming-out party due to the war, I'd heard, so her mother must have been making up for it with this big and lavish event. There had to have been close to two hundred people there.

I stood in the corner, alone, when Tom came in. Confident, smiling, a girl on his arm, he barely looked at me. Then Mrs. March brought him over after the girl wandered off to talk to some friends.

"This is my cousin's boy from Chicago, Thomas Buchanan," she said. "He's here for the wedding."

When she left us alone, he poured me some punch and proceeded to spike his with some liquor, which he also offered to me. I accepted. I accepted another after that, and soon we were laughing; I hadn't laughed in months! We escaped the chill of that vast parlor, and he drove me in a smart cruiser down to the river, where he became very fresh, and I became very loose.

I missed Jay. I thought he was never coming back. I thought he was gone, like Helen's fiancé, like so many others. I was tired of being despondent. I let Tom take me, on our very first meeting, even though my heart wasn't in it.

Tom not only stayed for the wedding. He lingered in Louisville for weeks after that. He often came around to see me, and I was smart enough to know that it was my willingness to make love to him that probably drove his attraction.

We drank and had sex. That was our relationship. I was happy to lose myself in liquor then, though I stopped short of inebriation. That would come later. Drinking soothed the hurt of losing Jay.

When I asked Tom his plans for returning to Chicago, he said he would go back to see his family and then return to Louisville.

"Oh, what for?" I asked him. "What will bring you back here?"

"To get married," he said. "I'll return to marry."

"Marry?" I asked, surprised he was so bold about double-timing me and his fiancée, whoever she was. "Who will you marry? Do I know her?"

"Why, it's you, you silly little fool." He tapped my nose. "I'll marry you."

I scoffed, even attempted to walk away, but he held on to my hand and said, "Would that be so awful, Daisy? Marrying me? I'm not a bad man, you know."

He was true to his word. He courted me with a ferocity both charming and fearsome. He cheerfully showed up with flowers, chocolates, silk scarves, and jewelry. When he did return to Chicago, he wrote letter after letter, and in my mind they took the place of the ones I didn't get from Jay. The day after I read of a particularly ghastly battle in France, I took off the necklace with his ring and put it away permanently. I felt a fool for thinking he could possibly have survived.

I was convinced he was dead. Maybe at that point, I even wanted that to be the case. I just wanted to know, to be sure, so I could move on.

My mother and father liked Tom; he came from a respectable, well-established family.

"You could do much worse, and you can't wait forever," my mother told me one night. "Tom has spoken to your father."

I did love Tom. Not in the same open-hearted way I'd loved Jay, but more than I'd felt for Rupert or Andrew, and by then I'd heard that Rupert, too, was dead. He, of the poor eyesight and cartography skills, had been in a headquarters building in France when a German mortar hit it.

I cried over his death. I wept out all my grief for Jay. The very next day, Tom asked for my hand, and I enthusiastically said yes. Jay would want me to go on with life, I reasoned, and I temporarily put him out of my head.

When Tom proposed, it was at the club after a polo match he had played there, and he gave me a stunning diamond ring circled with emeralds and more diamonds. He'd intended on giving it to me at a romantic dinner later, he said, but his victory on the polo field had him feeling exuberant and ready to conquer the world, starting with me.

I no longer felt fresh and young. I felt a bit used up, and once, even Tom hinted we better be careful about our lovemaking, or people would gossip and my reputation would be ruined.

I had told Jay I wanted to be a princess. I couldn't very well do that without a prince, and Tom was as close to an American one as I would get. His family dated back to the Mayflower, had money by the bushel full, and a name that opened doors from Chicago to New York.

We made plans to marry quickly in the fall. Mother consulted Mrs. Dale, who selected a fine white silk dress with beaded embroidery on its dropped bodice and a filmy floor-length veil held in place by a white rose garland to adorn my head.

Our parlor would be the setting, and Jordan, with whom I'd become good friends the summer before, would be my maid of honor. Flowers were ordered, the menu planned, dinners held to introduce our families to each other. It all happened in a rush— from proposal to vows, a scant six weeks. In those days, fast weddings were as common as long engagements. No one begrudged a couple their happiness.

By this time sickness had crept into our lives. Helen Beaufort came down with the flu and died within a week. Lilith caught it and was bedridden for a month. Barely surviving, she became frail and oddly distant after. Candace too was afflicted, and though she survived, she seemed slower and gentler, no longer capable of the mental lists she had kept before.

DAISY

Death, it seemed, was everywhere, and if I wasn't reading obituaries of classmates killed in the war, I was hearing stories of civilian friends who had taken to their sick beds.

It didn't matter that the war was ending. Its scythe had cut down everything good in life.

Getting ready for the dinner the night before my nuptials, however, when I'd at last reasoned Jay was gone from my life, maybe from all life, a shock came, delivered by the postman a little before three. I'd awakened from a nap and gone downstairs to get a glass of lemonade before asking the maid to draw my bath.

It was unseasonably warm, even though it was fall, and the light coming through our front door's pebbled glass had an eerie golden-brown hue, as if the sun itself had become an autumn leaf, changing color for the season.

I remember hearing the clock strike the hour as I passed the little table in the foyer, and there, on top of the day's mail, was an envelope of the thinnest paper, with a military return address.

My heart raced. Though I'd long expected bad news about Jay, I faced its reality now. Sure to find a note from a friend telling me of Jay's death, I grabbed the envelope and rushed up the steps again, tears already burning my eyelids as I anticipated grief.

You knew this would happen, I told myself. At least you'll now be sure. You won't wonder any longer. At least that pain will be gone.

Mother was resting, and Father was running an errand. The help was elsewhere in our big house. I was alone.

I opened my bedroom door, went to the window seat overlooking the back garden, took a deep breath, and slit the envelope with my fingernail.

Tears came, flowing down my cheeks and spotting my mauve linen dress, as I read:

Dear Daisy,

Darling, can you believe it? I've been writing to you for months now and only just found out you weren't getting a single letter! When you stopped writing, I was sure something awful had happened, but then a nice lady across town from you wrote me back that no Daisy Faye lived at the address I was sending my letters to! She said she'd tried notifying the military, but word never came to me until recently.

I'm pretty sure I have the right address now and you'll write back. I have thought of you every day. It didn't take long to get "over here" after what seemed a year of training and waiting. Now everything is in a hurry and rumors abound that we're going home or facing battle again.

After I left you, I couldn't forget your forlorn face, and nothing on earth would make me happier than to see you again and hold you in my arms, sitting quiet and soft and sweet on the swing of your front porch.

I will be thinking of that time and you, in the days to come. If, God willing, I do come home alive and whole, I know you will still be there, waiting with open arms.

Can you imagine it, dear? Me in uniform with my kit bag walking up the steps to your door? Can you see yourself standing there and jumping up and down a little, the way you would when you got excited about something?

I can.

That's what holds my spirits up, and it's what, I'm sure, will keep me alive, knowing you'll be waiting when I return, just like you promised. Many fellows here don't have a girl back home, and I feel awfully sorry for them. They don't fight the same way as those of us with a girl to get back to. All of you ladies keep us going, and I think of you and kiss your picture every night— the same with that sweet lock of hair that still smells like your perfume— every time it looks like we're headed into battle....

I don't know how long I sat there, rereading his letter, thinking of what was to come—my wedding to Tom.

Jay was alive. He could still be in harm's way. And my fidelity was all it took to keep him alive.

I'd failed him.

At some point, as shadows became longer, as the clock chimed another hour, I bestirred myself. I ran downstairs and found a bottle of bourbon.

I simply couldn't marry Tom. I couldn't do it.

With shaking hands, I poured myself a tumbler. And then another. And another.

I cried some more. The maid came in, looked at me curiously, and said she'd draw my bath. I told her not to bother.

She scurried out of the room, and I heard her calling my mother.

At some point, Jordan arrived, and she looked at the nearly empty bottle of liquor and shook her head.

"Oh, Daisy," she said, and wrapped her arms around me. "Let's get you into a warm bath, shall we?"

Mother was in the room now too—how did she get there? Muddled by booze and grief, I couldn't keep track of time.

She and Jordan practically carried me upstairs, one on either side of me, Mother saying something about nervous brides and obligations, and Jordan whispering that it would be all right.

I let them shepherd me. I had no idea what was happening. Jordan said she would telephone to the hotel where Tom's family was staying to let them know we'd be late for the family dinner they'd planned that evening in the hotel restaurant. She went downstairs to place the call.

As I undressed, the doorbell rang. Soon, Jordan appeared in my bedroom, holding a blue velvet box decorated with a gold ribbon. I stood by my bed, naked, paralyzed, Jay's letter crumpled on the floor.

"It's from Tom," she said, and when I didn't move, she pulled at the bow and opened the box. A stunning pearl necklace lay on a satin cloth. Again, when I didn't move, she pulled out a note, and read a sweet message from Tom to go with this gift for his bride.

"I can't do it," I sobbed, now sitting on the bed, my head in my hands. "J-J-Jay's alive. Oh, God, he's still alive!"

Just as my mother came in the room, Jordan saw the letter on the floor and picked it up. She read it silently as my mother fussed.

"Daisy, you'll catch your death of cold! Here, let's get your robe." She brought over a pink silk kimono and pressed it around my shoulders. "Your bath is ready."

She walked me to the bathroom, Jordan following.

"I'll stay with her, Mrs. Faye," she said softly, and closed the door. Like an automaton, I moved forward and slid into the sudsy bath, wanting to sink below its surface and not have to think at all.

"I can't do it," I repeated, not to her, but to the room, to the universe. "If I marry Tom, Jay will die!"

"Oh, Daisy, what nonsense," Jordan said, pulling up a cushioned chair, and placing her hand on my arm. "Look at me."

Turning my head slowly, I peered into her eyes. "You read the letter. He thinks of me. I keep him alive. What will happen when he learns I..." I couldn't finish it.

"Nothing will happen. You don't even know what's happening now. Listen to me, Daisy. You will marry Tom. You will be happy. Jay will be happy, too. He will live or not and it won't have a single thing to do with you. Not a thing."

"But—"

"You can't ruin your life because of one letter. Stay true to your promise to Tom. I know you love him. You told me so."

I had told Jordan that, but I think I did so to convince myself it was true. When I thought Jay was gone for good, I'd consciously moved my affection to Tom.

"Think of that—how you have come to love Tom. Don't toss that aside for one letter. For all you know..."

"Don't say it!" I shouted. "I won't think Jay's dead again. I won't!"

Undaunted, she went on: "Tom adores you."

From the hall, my mother's voice called, "Is everything all right? We need to be going soon."

At that, Jordan picked up a washcloth and started bathing me, as if I were a child, her gentle hands caressing my body as I closed my eyes and tried to gather rational thoughts. None would come.

Eventually, she helped me stand and dried me off, then brushed my hair. Jordan could be very tender underneath her gruff exterior, and she treated me as if I were a fragile invalid, offering cooing encouragement.

She led me back to my room, while my mother, her brow furrowed, stood silently outside in the hall. Then she helped me dress. When she put Tom's pearls around my neck, though, I couldn't bear it, and yanked them free. They scattered to the floor.

Jordan didn't judge. She didn't even cluck her tongue. "He can buy you another one." She stepped back and gazed at me. "There, you look beautiful. We'll tell Tom you've been suffering from a headache, but, Daisy, you will get through this. It's one night and one day, and then...then you can decide what to do. For now, marry Tom. Don't ruin your life."

Somehow I did get through it—the dinner that night, the wedding the next day. Jordan's words—*don't ruin your life*—echoed in my heart and mind every moment. When I was about to falter, she would appear by my elbow and whisper encouragement or ask how I was feeling. For all Tom's family knew, I was suffering from a splitting headache.

I had never felt such a burden before. It was as if, with every step I took up the aisle to wed Tom, I would be firing the shots that would surely kill that loyal soldier, Jay.

My fidelity was the only cost of keeping him alive—my true love, which I so recklessly promised him and then threw to Tom when I was afraid no one decent would be left to take it.

It was the one hard thing I had been asked to do in my easy life so far, the one thing that required courage—wait for Jay. Yet I'd failed in that task. Failed miserably.

Other women waited patiently for their loves to return from war. Why hadn't I been able to do so, too?

This revelation made me sick with self-loathing, and part of me wondered if my punishment was this marriage. I had allowed Tom to buy me, with a promise of safety, security, and peace. The pearls were just a symbol of that price.

Mother and Jordan worked hard to help me recover and be presentable that evening and the next day. At some point, I knew Mother had seen the letter. I think she assumed it stayed in the trash bin, but I'd retrieved it after the dinner party was over, flattened it out, wept some more, kissed my fingers to it, then folded it neatly and shoved it into a far corner of my luggage.

I knew I had to marry Tom. And I felt I was dooming Jay by doing so. I consoled myself by thinking I'd not answer Jay's letter, not tell him of my marriage, and if he should write again—which he did—Mother could send him the news of the wedding. She would know what to say.

So, I married, had the largest and most glamorous reception afterward, then went on a honeymoon, where I forced the past into a box I refused to open. I forced myself to fall in love with Tom.

When we returned to Louisville all tanned and happy for a post-honeymoon visit, my mother took me aside and said she had "taken care of the matter, and that man would not bother me again."

CHAPTER EIGHT

N ow I read the letter again in my bathroom, sitting on the gilt vanity chair, door latched, the present and future locked out, only the past intruding.

It still bore the wrinkled marks of the crumpling I'd given it, and a lot of the ink was smeared from bathwater.

This past week, Jay told me what my mother had done to deter him from pursuing me further. She'd sent him clippings of our wedding—it had been written up in major newspapers—and told him, in the sweetest note, he said, that I was married and happy and she'd not given me his pleading letter for fear of upsetting me. My mother, a devout Methodist who never missed church, told an outright lie.

A lie I compounded, of course, by being deliberately vague when Jay asked me if I had received it. So he still believed my mother's story was true, that the letter had "arrived" the night before my wedding, but I'd not seen his heartfelt plea, I'd not deliberately and consciously rejected him. I'm not sure precisely what else he believed. I was too afraid to ask. All he admitted was that he was "mighty disappointed" to hear of my marriage and assumed it was an arranged thing. I didn't disabuse him of that lie.

Why couldn't I be honest with him? With any man? With myself? I wanted to be. I wanted to stay true.

DAISY

Jordan had cautioned me not to ruin my life when she'd urged me to go through with the wedding to Tom. However, it felt as if I'd done that very thing. I'd ruined it by not waiting for Jay.

Pulling myself together, I stood, a resolution forming in my mind. Still holding the crumpled letter, I went back into my bedroom and gazed at my wedding photograph on the dresser by the door. In it, Tom stood straight and proud, his arm looped through mine. I looked pale and ill, but there was more than one reason for that and it was not just Jay's untimely letter or the knowledge he had written many more I'd never received.

My dress was simple and loose for good reason. I had been expecting our first child. Jordan had known, and my mother suspected.

I lost that baby at five months, shortly after our honeymoon, and the doctor told me then I was unlikely to carry a child to term after that.

He was wrong, and when Pamela was conceived, I was filled with joy and fear. Tom's ardor for me had waned considerably by then, so it was only by great luck that his passion burned at the right moment and darling Pammy was the result. I determined to do everything in my power to make sure this child thrived.

I also knew by then that my marriage to Tom was less than perfect. I knew he found pleasure in other women's arms, and I felt like a fool for not realizing this would be my fate, to be the betrayed wife. After all, he'd quickly bedded me. Why would he have any reservations about taking other women he wanted? It was a habit of his.

We had traveled to Europe by then, and he'd had a lover or two while there, I was sure, judging by the smug glances he sent to singers in smoky jazz clubs and a young female reporter we met at a dinner in Paris.

Yet, I stayed true. I decided that I would never give myself so freely again, that Tom was my husband, and I would remain faithful. I embraced it with the zeal of a religious convert. It was a form of revenge: to be what he couldn't be. I knew he was aware of my virtue and resented it.

But I knew he'd resent my infidelity to him even more.

At least I had Pamela. That beautiful creature had come from all this turmoil.

A sob crawled up my throat and almost choked me, and reflexively I felt my hand crumpling the letter once more into a ball. I let out a feral cry and ripped the paper into little pieces, not wanting it to haunt me any longer.

Then I pulled the photograph from its silver frame and consigned it to the same fate, its waxy fragments joining Jay's letter in the trash bin.

The past thus destroyed, I drew my own bath and sank into a field of lavender bubbles, where I stayed until I declined the request to come down to dinner.

Jordan was right. I needed to make a plan. With details, not just vague notions.

DAISY

Tomorrow afternoon, I'd ring up Nick and this time, I would be the one arranging the rendezvous at his home. For me, him, Jay…and Pamela.

(HAPTER NINE

I t was dismal. Not the weather this time, but the atmosphere—the day I'd set up a meeting with Jay at Nick's so he could meet my daughter, maybe even come to love her.

I'd brought a few playthings with me for Pamela to enjoy, but she was in a fussy mood that afternoon. We were meeting during her usual nap time because of when I could get away without Tom knowing what I was doing.

I'd told Tom that Pamela's "Uncle Nick" had proposed a tea party for her, and gushed over how thoughtful it was of my cousin to treat our sweet little princess, and I hope he didn't mind but I'd told Nick I didn't think Tom would be interested in coming. I held my breath until Tom nodded over his morning paper and then went out for the rest of the day.

I dressed Pammy in one of her sweetest dresses, a white smock with embroidered blue rocking horses around the hem and a "Peter Pan" collar and blue bow tie with long ribbons ending in blue beads. I combed her feathery blond hair and secured it with a silver butterfly barrette, though I knew it was unlikely to stay in place for long. She had my fine, wispy hair, which had been an annoyance for my own nanny when I was young.

She was as pretty as could be, and I was proud of her, and when Jay first set eyes on her as we walked up to Nick's cottage, I was pleased to see him grinning in genuine appreciation. At least the afternoon got off to a good start.

Even under the best of circumstances, though, having a social event with children underfoot presents a challenge. Children were usually sent away to play after a short appearance among guests. You could then be admired for producing such beautiful offspring without being bothered by the messiness and noise of having them nearby.

Yet here we were, trapped for at least an hour with nowhere for Pamela to go and conversation difficult, as she often interrupted, or I had to see to her.

Jay sat awkwardly on the settee and tried to talk with her.

"You're a pretty little thing," he said, smiling, his hands on his knees. "You look just like your mother."

Pamela responded with silence as she positioned a brightly colored block on top of another, then pouted when they both fell, and wailed when she hit her head on the table's edge as she tried to retrieve the bunch.

After picking her up to soothe her, I placed her in my lap.

"There, there, sweetie. It's nothing. We all fall sometimes." I kissed her head and looked over at Jay. "Actually, she has Tom's eyes," I said.

At that observation, Jay recoiled. It was just the slightest movement, a little crinkling about his eyes and pulling back, but I saw it.

Nick, who was our host, came into the room with a tray of treats—some cookies and small cakes—and a pot of tea. He did not put into use the beautiful rose and gold china of my first meeting here with Jay, but a sturdier white porcelain with no adornment.

"Would you like some, honey?" I asked, and she nodded, still sniffling over her recent hurt.

If I had thought this part of the day would go more smoothly, I was quickly disappointed. Despite my best efforts, Pammy spilled her tea after first almost burning herself on it because it was too hot. This elicited a comment from Jay that she had ruined her pretty dress. At that, she pouted and cried. Then she insisted on having more cakes than I told her she could have, and in the interest of peace, I gave in to her demand.

"You should listen to your mother," Jay announced, as she reached for an iced sweet. "You'll get a stomach ache if you don't."

She popped the cake in her mouth and looked at him as if he were the most foolish man on earth.

After that, she decided to explore Nick's home and toddled off down the hallway. A crash soon followed, and when I ran to fetch her, I saw she had pulled at a towel on the kitchen table, resulting in a pile of cutlery landing on the floor, which she seemed to think were toys meant just for her. Upon returning to the parlor, I scooped her up with some spoons that occupied her for a little while.

By the time the hour was over, I could hardly wait to leave. Jay eventually gave up trying to interact with Pamela and instead ended up treating the appointment as if I were there alone, or rather, just with Nick.

But as he started conversations about stocks, news, music, or his car, Pamela would somehow always manage to grab my attention, and I would have to tend to her, keep her from going out the door, and follow her as she wanted to explore Nick's house again, asking questions.

I was frazzled and eager to leave when I finally picked her up and headed for the door, and I could tell that Jay had enjoyed our get-together as little as I had.

As we said farewell, he started to lean toward me to give me a kiss, but I pulled back and offered my hand, nodding toward Pamela, who would surely report a kiss to Daddy at some point in her garbled-toddler language. He understood but grimaced, and then said he hoped to see me soon.

The only thing that saved the event from being a complete failure was Pamela's farewell. She gave Jay a big grin and waved at him, without prompting. It gave me some hope that we could all enjoy being together sometime soon, after they got to know each other better.

The next afternoon, I did see Jay alone, and we didn't say a word about his session with Pamela. I didn't bring it up, and he acted as if it hadn't even happened. Once again, I lacked courage.

But by avoiding the subject, our hours together were unblemished by discord. I was an expert at pushing away conflict, even if part of me worried it would resurface at some time, that in fact it needed to resurface.

I left that day's rendezvous happy and hopeful, my skin still tingling from his touch, determined to try again to bring him round to loving Pamela as much as he loved me.

You see, as much as Tom liked Pammy to be out of his way, there was no doubt how much he loved her. His eyes lit up whenever he saw her. He seemed proud to have brought into the world such a sweet, beautiful creature.

I had to know Jay would one day feel the same about Pammy, and I approached it like an ordinary task.

Other tasks intruded, however, in the coming days. Specifically, how to stay out of the madhouse.

CHAPTER TEN

As I fell ever more deeply in love with Jay, I decided I needed to work harder to hide my ecstasy from Tom. He always seemed less suspicious if I was unhappy.

So several mornings I faked swooning about, seemingly uninterested in even getting out of bed, and powdering my face to an ashy pale shade.

But I couldn't hide everything I was feeling, and just two days after the tea at Nick's with Pamela and Jay, all the tension of my secret affair, my doubts, and my fears spilled over.

It started with a call from Myrtle. I heard the whole thing. I had picked up the phone just after Tom took the call, and listened in upstairs in my room.

Oh, the cooing from him, the low-class nagging from her, and when he said he might not be able to get away that day, her reply sent an arrow to my heart:

"Oh, Tommy baby, I misses you so much," she said in a simpering baby voice. "And I have some news to tell you. Babykins hasn't been feeling so well lately, and I might need to go to the doctor."

I heard Tom inhale sharply.

I grasped the phone, my fingers turning white from my grip.

"Myrtle, now, you know you have these agues…"

"Oh, it ain't no ague, sweetheart. Aren't you excited? I didn't want to say it on the phone, but you could be a daddy!"

"He was a daddy," I wanted to shout at the insolent bitch.

"But you said you didn't go to the doctor yet?" he asked in a desperate voice. "So it might be a false alarm, darling."

An awful sound came over the line, and I realized she was crying.

"T-t-tom," she stuttered. "Don't be so mean to me. Come and see me, please. I don't know what I'll do if you don't come…"

"All right, all right. Let me see what I can do."

I hung up as soon as I heard his click, and I sat on the edge of the bed, seething.

Tears burned my eyes, but I shook my head and willed them away.

His mistress pregnant with his bastard?

Never! No one would threaten my daughter's place in his dynasty such as it was.

I was furious even at the possibility. I was a good mother. It was part of who I was now. I was Daisy Faye Buchanan, mother. Not just a lover. My attempt to get Jay to understand that failed. Now the father of my child was conspiring with another woman to displace that child? Never.

Rising, I paced to the window. I felt imprisoned. Earlier, I had hoped he'd go out for the afternoon. Now I didn't want him to. I wanted him to stay here and suffer, just like me.

I wanted to be the one racing out—over to Jay's, to tell him of this awful occurrence, and to have him reassure me that he would see to Pammy's future.

A soft knock at my door.

"Daisy? Are you awake?" Tom said through the door.

"I'm not feeling well," I said, no longer having to pretend to be upset.

"I'll be going into town. Business meeting. Don't hold dinner."

He sounded so casual, so unconcerned about me. The scoundrel.

Without thinking, I hurried to the door, threw it open, and pummeled my fists on his chest.

He grabbed my wrists and held them still. He cocked his head to one side and peered at me.

"Daisy, what on earth is the matter with you? Are you all right?"

"No, no, I'm not! Where are you going?"

"Just into town. Nothing to concern yourself with," he said, peering at me again as if searching for signs of illness.

"I want to go into town!" I said. I didn't, of course, but I was so damned tired of Tom being able to do whatever the hell he wanted while I had to pretend to be sick, and devise plans to fool him, plan to sneak out, even when he was away. I wanted that same freedom. He could drive off by simply announcing he was doing so. "Let me get a wrap," I said. "We can go together."

I managed to pull away and step back into my room, where I grabbed a bag as if to leave. While I was turned away, he closed the door. And locked it.

"You're not well, dear. You need to stay home. I'll call the doctor for you."

I stomped to the door, jiggling the knob to no avail. Its lock operated with a key on either side. Mine was gone.

Growling, I picked up the nearest object, my bedside lamp, and threw it at the door.

That loud crash provided me such satisfaction that I decided to replicate it. Destroying the things that showcased our wealth made me shiver with delight. I went round the room and smashed every piece of porcelain or china or glass I could find. Expensive figurines, lamps, a Wedgwood hairpin case.

I threw them at the walls, the mirror, which I also cracked, and then tossed shoes and clothes into my bathtub and lit a match to the pile. I wanted to dispose of it all, these signs of indulgence and luxury. Maybe if I literally burned them all, I would be able to walk away from what they offered me.

"Daisy! What's burning? Daisy?!" he yelled at last, and then the door opened, and he entered. He said nothing at first, just looked around, his mouth set in fury, his eyes slit. Then he glanced at the dying flames in the nearby bath and called for the maid.

"Bring buckets of water!" he shouted. By then, my little conflagration had nearly extinguished itself on its own, but soon a maid and the housekeeper rushed in and killed the embers with splashes of water.

At that moment, Nanny walked by with Pammy, now back from an outing. When she saw the scene, she started crying, then wailing and screaming, wanting to know what happened.

"Take her to her room," Tom instructed, waving his hand to indicate Pamela should be pulled away.

"Call Doctor Prinz," Tom told the housekeeper. He gave me a look of utter disgust but still left. My fit did nothing to keep him from going to his mistress. It just meant I couldn't go to my lover.

While unsuccessful in getting Tom to stay home, I did manage to get a syringe of some sort of sedative pumped into me within the hour, and it set me free in an odd way. Dr. Prinz, a middle-aged physician who prided himself on staying up to date with all the latest treatments, informed me that he would speak to my husband about "next steps." That sounded ominous.

Whatever he gave me had me floating over to Jay's through the clouds, and I fell into a dreamy sleep, where I imagined Jay making love to me throughout the night.

I must have been quite vocal during this hallucinatory love-making because the next morning, I heard Tom and Dr. Prinz outside my bedroom, after he had checked on me, talking about my "hypersexualized fantasies."

This had an undesirable effect.

Whatever Tom's situation with Myrtle, he must have decided that I was no longer a goddess if I could have such carnal thoughts, and he didn't try to beckon me to his bed. He came to mine three nights in a row.

No matter how many times I told him I wasn't in the mood for anything, he ignored me. I could lie there like a corpse, and that just seemed to fuel his passion.

These sessions left me truly ill and haggard each morning. I couldn't imagine going to Jay's because I felt I'd betrayed him and he would see it in my face, seen I had not been able to fend Tom off.

So now I became miserable. There was no need for pretense.

I didn't care if Myrtle was pregnant. At that point, I wanted Tom to go to her and promise her his undying love, as long as it would keep him away from me.

At last, after five days of imprisonment, I was set free.

Tom went into town and announced he'd not be back until the next day.

I bathed. I dressed in one of the new outfits he delivered to replace my burnt ones, and I drove to Jay's.

I'd reclaim myself, even if now the pretense was acting sane, not mad.

"I'll kill him," Jay said in a low, angry voice I'd never heard him use. His fists clenched by my side as we lay in his bed together.

I'd wanted Jay's lovemaking to purify me in some way. His gentle and sweet kisses healed me.

But my bruises remained, and when he asked me how I'd gotten the ones visible on my wrists and arms, I told him simply that Tom had held me down.

"Down for what?" he asked.

I looked away and didn't answer.

He rose from the bed, grabbed a cigarette and robe, and went to the window to look at the Sound, or perhaps at our house across the way.

After smoking for a moment, he said, without looking at me. "You know Tom double-crossed Anthony."

"Anthony?" I sat up and reached for a cigarette for myself.

When he heard me stir, Jay came to the bed and lit the smoke for me.

"Delacorte. The man you met at one of my parties, who helped me get new staff here." He waved his smoke in the direction of the door.

Ah, the gangster.

"How'd he do that? Double cross him, I mean," I asked. I couldn't imagine Tom even knowing how to do such a thing.

"He promised he'd buy a truckload of liquor and then reneged on the deal. Tony told him he had to pay up, but then just as he thought he might have to cut his losses and sell it elsewhere, his driver was arrested and the whole shipment tossed. Somebody must have tipped off the cops. Tony thinks it was Tom, not wanting to pay." Jay blew a plume of smoke into the air. "I calmed him down."

"You did?"

He nodded and sat next to me on the bed, stroking my arm. "Maybe I shouldn't have."

For a long moment, I held my breath. I wondered what gangsters did when they were double-crossed. I wanted to ask, but I didn't want to know. I think I already knew.

So all I did was offer a small nod.

"All right then," Jay said, as if we'd decided something. "I'll tell Tony I was wrong."

I managed to convince Dr. Prinz to tell Tom to leave me alone.

During his next check on me the following morning, I had the chance to talk to him privately. Tom was still out.

I played the demure wife, a woman whose knowledge of worldly things is limited. I looked down bashfully, picking at my robe when I talked, and signaling my embarrassment.

And I told him my husband made me do things I didn't want to do.

I broke down crying, and before long, the tears were real, and I was having a very genuine attack of hysteria.

Dr. Prinz was convinced. He wanted to give me another sedative, but I recovered by then and said no; I wanted to regain my strength, to become capable again, especially to be a good mother once more.

Having heard intimate details he didn't want to hear, he stood, red-faced, and told me he would talk to Mr. Buchanan about how much I needed rest. Complete rest.

Tom not only left me alone after that, he went into town more frequently, so this strategy turned out to be doubly beneficial.

By now I was committed to leaving him and no longer had any doubts. I merely had to construct the plan that Jordan had strongly recommended. As I saw it, part of the plan was to ensure Jay's devotion to Pamela and to making sure I'd be able to keep her with me when I left my brute of a husband.

CHAPTER ELEVEN

Throughout that summer, I accumulated cash. I had never thought about it much before—never had to. Tom usually gave me whatever I asked for and more, really: a monthly allotment for odds and ends. Most of our bills were paid by check, by tabs we'd run up at stores and with other services.

So I'd never had to think much about money, about what it cost to live in the world. I went from a household where my father would buy me whatever I wanted to a home where my husband would do the same.

I began arming myself with information, again letting Tom school me on such matters during dinner conversations where I would start by asking why the lower races didn't just live in better neighborhoods instead of the squalor of tenements.

Then I'd be treated to a lecture on those races' natural inferiority, but it would give me the chance to ask specific questions about how much one paid in rent or for a car, gasoline, food, and the like.

I had to be careful, though. After one such dinner, while Tom was replenishing our drinks, Jordan whispered to me on the veranda, "Careful, dear, you don't want to be too obvious."

So I made sure to guide our talk back to the latest Broadway hit, which we all agreed was silly even though none of us had seen it. We did that a lot—talked critically of things we had never experienced. It seemed to bring us joy. It brought Tom even greater joy when he could simultaneously sneer at something while also poking fun at my similar opinions about the same thing.

I'd progressively accumulate this knowledge, and I would often jot random numbers down in my room, only to have difficulty deciphering them later.

When I complained to Jordan about how hard it was to accumulate cash, to even know how much to save, she sat back and laughed.

We were having lobster salad on a perfect summer day, sun glinting off the water while a soft breeze blew the curtains in a gentle dance around the veranda, just the two of us there, a girls' luncheon.

"Frankly, I'm not sure why you're bothering with all this. Gatsby is rich as Croesus. You will be going from one well-feathered nest to another. Why worry about it?"

This was true, but something in me wanted to feel secure on my own. No man would ever be able to lock me in a room again.

"I know," I said, looking out over the Sound, toward Jay's house, something I did more and more often. He was away at the moment, on some kind of business trip upstate. It was the first time we hadn't been in the same locale since beginning our summer affair. Even during my recent confinement, I'd still known he was there across the water, just waiting for me. Now I'd not hear from him until Thursday. It made me fearful.

"These things are complicated," I said at last. "What if Tom tries to ruin me, or ruin Jay? What if everything comes crashing down on us?"

Jordan smiled and pulled out a smoke, which she had trouble lighting in the breeze. When she finally had it going, she took a drag on it, judged it of poor quality, and stubbed it out.

"If everything came crashing down, no budget prowess will help you. We'd all be in the same trouble then. So again, why worry about it?"

I did worry about it, though, especially when I thought of Jordan mentioning the possibility the whole thing could come crashing down on all of us. Anyone who lived through those crazy times knows there was always an air of "eat, drink, and be merry, for tomorrow we die" to them. It started with the end of the war, of course. When that horrible rupture was over and we all regarded the smoking landscapes and the men with ripped faces and brutalized psyches, how could we not feel that you had to grab each day and squeeze the last drop of pleasure out of it whenever you could?

None of us listened to supplications for moderation. Not even Prohibition dampened our desire for more booze. We wanted more of everything—more fun, more music, more dancing, more money.

In fact, if I had to choose one word to describe those years, it would be scandalous.

Clothing was scandalous.

Haircuts were scandalous.

DAISY

Dances were scandalous.

About the only thing that didn't seem scandalous were actual scandals. Phrases like "Teapot Dome" and "gold digger" flitted through newspaper stories like gnats to be swatted away.

Peggy Hopkins Joyce was on her third marriage—or was it her fourth?—and while old doyennes may have gasped at the actress's shameless couplings with any available rich man, I'm sure many a shop girl thought it wasn't a bad idea.

Boredom was now counted among the seven deadly sins, and the others included prudishness, moderation, false humility, diligence, seriousness, and self-denial.

I had felt I was missing out on life since I married, and now, with Jay, I was in it again.

Jay returned from his business trip early, and as luck would have it, it was the very same day that Tom decided to stay home, forgoing the pleasures of stout "Babykins" Myrtle. I didn't know if she was with child, and I didn't care. If I left Tom, he could have all the bastards he wanted. He could have a whole tribe of them.

As he sat reading the newspaper in the dining room that Wednesday morning, I sat upstairs on my bed, scratching numbers on a piece of paper again, figuring out how much I needed for monthly expenses and how much I had stashed away.

From my reckoning, I had enough cash for four months of living on my own in a modest apartment somewhere. Jordan had told me that costs would be lower everywhere but New York.

I knew she was right about Jay's wealth, and I had no doubt he would spoil me with anything I wanted after we came together permanently, but I still had this nagging sense it was best to plan a life on my own. I knew definitely I wanted to leave Tom. But being with Jay forever? A fog of uncertainty blocked me from seeing that future clearly. I wanted to plan for contingencies.

Perhaps the easiest route was for me to leave Tom, live alone with Pamela for a while, divorce Tom, and then be with Jay. I could handle all that without help, without support from either man that could end up slowing proceedings.

I'd still not talked to Jay at length about Pamela. I just couldn't bring myself to ruin our golden hours with anything that would diminish our happiness.

Pamela was in the sunroom with Nanny when Jay pulled up the drive. I heard the gravel crunch and looked outside, my heart racing as I saw his dashing figure get out of that bold bright car of his.

After quickly running my fingers through my hair and applying a coat of lipstick, I ran down the steps to the door before he could even ring the bell.

"I couldn't wait to see you," he whispered, peering beyond me to make sure we were alone.

"I missed you, too," I said. Then I took a chance and leaned in to kiss him lightly on the cheek.

It was then that Pammy came into the hall. When she saw Jay, she walked forward, grinning. She wasn't a shy child. Like me, she was happy to be around people, and already she had a good memory for those she met.

"Miss'er Gabby," she slurred and then ran toward him, obviously expecting him to pick her up. My heart lifted. She remembered him. Fondly.

Surprisingly, he did pick her up, grinning at me as if to say, "now look at this."

That's when Tom joined us.

"What's this?" he said, taking in our little domestic tableaux, but squinting with confusion and doubt.

I reached over and grabbed Pammy, kissing her on the forehead before putting her down and instructing her, "Go find Nanny, dear." She toddled off as Nanny came round the corner of the hall for her.

"Hello, old sport," Jay said, holding his hand out to Tom. "I've been away and was driving back. Before I headed over to West Egg, thought I'd stop by to discuss some good deals with you."

Tom frowned, and at that moment I noticed the tiniest speck of my lipstick on Jay's cheek. Though it was hardly more than a pinprick's diameter, it seemed a flashing red sign to me, and I kept my face away from Tom so he wouldn't notice it was the same shade I was wearing.

"I'm not sure I'm up for that today, old boy," Tom said, emphasizing the last two words, as if mocking Jay. "Come round another time, will you?" It was as if he were dismissing a tradesman.

I still dared not turn completely to face Tom. So I laughed and said, "Tom's out of sorts today. Here, let me see your car." And I walked down the steps toward it. "Tom, would you check on Pamela?" I asked without turning around. After a moment, I heard him retreat into the house.

At his vehicle, I whispered to Jay, "I can come by tomorrow, I think."

"Not today?" he said, his voice filled with longing.

I shook my head. "Tom's moping about for some reason. Maybe Myrtle threw him over."

Jay laughed. "Don't think so. I've heard she's getting a little, well, plumper. He might not like being tied to her and her litter."

My face warmed, and I knew my cheeks were blazing. So she *was* pregnant. How many people knew if Jay did?

Filled with anger, I said, "Wait right here."

I stomped up the steps, opened the door, and called out, "Tom! Jay is taking me for a drive in his car!"

Later, in bed with him, warm from lovemaking, our reunion complete, I watched as Jay rolled on his side and propped his head on his elbow.

"I did come by to talk about a deal," he said seriously. "The one I mentioned, with the associate of Anthony Delacorte's." His gaze probed me for doubt, but I had none that I cared to think about.

I let out a long sigh and stared at the ceiling. "I wish we could just go. Now. You and me. To Europe. To the other side of the world. To somewhere where there isn't a single Tom or Thomas around, where his name is banned for all eternity."

He let out a low chuckle and kissed me.

"All right. Let's." He actually got out of bed, as if he was going to make the arrangements then and there.

He pulled on his trousers and a shirt and was about to reach for the phone, when I said, "Stop!" while laughing at his impulsiveness. "We can't. *I* can't."

After putting the phone down, he turned to me, smile still on his face. "Why not? It's perfect. He won't even realize you're gone until we're far away, and then it will be too late to find us. You don't need anything. I'll buy you a new wardrobe. I'll buy you new everything." He snapped his fingers as if he could make items appear instantly.

"Oh, Jay. That's so sweet." I sat up, pulling the sheet to my shoulders. I'd have to go soon. Despite what Jay had said, Tom was probably wondering at that moment why I had been away so long.

Jay came over to me, sat on the bed, and took my hands in his.

"Why not, Daisy? Come with me. Please. Now. We can do it." He kissed me, and in that kiss, I became so lost that I almost agreed to his crazy scheme. But after we separated, I uttered a single name.

"Pamela."

He sighed.

"I can't leave her," I said. Now I was the one reaching for his hand, comforting him. "I was so happy when she went to you today. It made me think…we could be together. All of us."

When I didn't say more, he spoke. "You doubted it? That we could all be together?"

"No, no," I said, shaking my head and knowing he would hear the insincerity. "It's just that I can't leave without Pamela."

"You can send for her."

I shook my head again. "Tom would never allow that. If I run away, he'll use her to punish me. I'd never see her again." Simply articulating that possibility made me shudder.

He stroked my cheek with his knuckles. "You're all I need," he said.

The implication was clear. He needed only me. Why didn't I need only him?

"I won't be your Anna," I said, forcing a firmness into my voice I had trouble mustering. "I won't forsake my child for you." I held my breath in this moment of honesty. This was new for me, to be utterly truthful with a man. It was the first bit of courage I had shown, and for a few seconds, it thrilled me.

His eyes widened, and I wondered if I needed to explain the Tolstoy reference, but then he leaned over and patted my hand and said, "We can have other children, Daisy. Many children. A garden of them." As if it was as easy as putting seeds into the earth and watching them grow.

"No, we can't," I said. "I can't anymore."

He surprised me by expressing no disappointment at all at this. If anything, he seemed happy to hear it. It hadn't shocked me when I'd first been told, but lately, I did find myself wondering if more children would somehow give my life the meaning I continued to crave.

"Oh, darling, that's just fine. More than fine. Really. I want only you. Children? No children? It doesn't matter to me. You're all that matters to me. Since the moment I met you, I knew I wanted you and you alone."

Me alone. There was a day when those words would have exhilarated me, when a lover whispering them would have filled me with light, warmth radiating from the inside.

Tom may never have uttered those words to me, but there had been a time when I knew he had wanted only me and me alone, too. I found out soon enough that once he'd made his conquest, his life seemed to lose meaning, a little more with each passing year. I wondered if this would happen to Jay once he had what he'd been seeking for so long.

But I had Pamela now. There was no me alone. There was me *and* Pamela.

When she was two, shortly after we returned from Europe, she came down with a ghastly fever. For five days, she lay abed, and I thought it was that dreadful infantile paralysis. I thought we'd lose her. Despite Tom's protests, I slept by her bed every night until the fever subsided and the doctor pronounced her recovered.

In those moments at her bedside, I realized I would be broken forever if I lost her. I'd never recover from that.

Now my heart broke anew. I felt the shards course through my veins, cutting every part of my being and entering my very soul. I wondered why I couldn't be honest with a man and have him accept that truth, instead of always needing to pretend, to jolly, to tease, to amuse.

I looked at him, willing him to say he would wait until I could make sure Pamela could be with us. I longed for those words. *Yes, darling, we absolutely must wait until we can have Pamela with us. There is no question we should wait.* But he merely smiled.

This sweet man, this darling man who'd followed me and wanted me and cherished me. Why? Why put in all that effort, devote all that time to this one mission—finding and winning his Daisy again? What had been missing from his life that he wanted me to fill? It was too much to ask of me or anyone, and I knew I'd eventually disappoint him, just as I had disappointed Tom.

With a shiver, I realized Jay was little different than Tom. He wanted a pretty object, a porcelain sculpture to put on his shelf, to look at and admire, to occasionally show off, and, yes, to love. Daisy alone, with no entanglements, no pesky children to change her into a plump matron. Just me.

What would happen when my beauty faded?

With a flash of more painful insight, I realized I was complicit in this. All the things I'd wanted from life I had gotten by playing that porcelain figurine. I'd bent in that same charming way toward men. I had lidded my eyes, bitten my tongue, looked shyly away, come up with clever lines, ceased being in any way intimidating. All so they'd love me. So Jay would love me now that I had lost Tom's love.

"We don't need more children. It can be just the two of us," he said, still smiling.

"Three," I reminded him, crushed he had already forgotten about the importance of my daughter. "The three of us."

"Yes, yes, of course."

With a massive effort, I once more became the porcelain figurine, smiling sweetly at him. "I need to get back. We might not be able to run away today, but we can plan our getaway. It will be the most fun of all, making arrangements for where we'll go, hotels we'll stay in, things we'll do..." I recited the lines as if from a play. I wanted to believe them, but something had changed.

We both dressed—I was very careful not to have a thread out of place—and walked to his car. By the time I got home, Tom had decided to go out, too, apparently, so there was no need for me to worry about an interrogation upon my return.

After I made my way up to my room, I realized I'd never given Jay any indication I wanted the contract with Mr. Delacorte changed, and now a wave of guilt washed over me.

CHAPTER TWELVE

Tom didn't come home that night. I knew he'd gone to see the Wilson woman, so I felt both relieved and angry. I was still feeling bruised by Jay's indifference toward my daughter, his refusal to acknowledge my feelings about her, and now I was confronted with a husband who might have sired another heir, someone who might eventually pose a challenge to my daughter's inheritance. Could neither man be bothered to look out for my child? I was infuriated and confused.

I had little time to make sense of these feelings because they were soon replaced by another emotion: fear. The next morning at breakfast, Tom commented on Jay's visit, and it was clear he had been stewing about it.

"Why does he have to stop by here? It's as if he thinks he's one of us."

I stopped buttering my toast and stared at him. "He came to discuss a deal with you. Weren't you doing deals with him?" I held my breath, hoping that by going on the offensive, I put him on the defensive, and he would stop thinking about why else Jay might have visited our house.

He waved his hand in the air. "Liquor. Everyone does that. Nothing special. And I stopped after a bad shipment." He stared back at me. "Was there something else he wanted?"

Tom was hardly subtle. He enjoyed feeling part of the hustle and bustle of business, of "deals," of buying bootleg liquor. But he always snapped back to his core nature, that of wealthy gentry, disdainful of anyone outside his elite set, especially if they tried too hard to get inside and take what was his.

"He did mention wanting to show you his car," I said, staring at him without batting an eye, trying to convey through an exaggerated calm that nothing was amiss. "But you were in a mood, so I did the polite thing and accompanied him for a drive."

He snorted. "The polite thing." After a pause, he said, "If I ever thought he—or any man—was taking advantage of my good graces to make a play for what isn't his, there will be hell to pay."

He went back to reading his newspaper.

I knew who would suffer that hell he promised. Me.

At least I knew where things stood. He suspected something between me and Jay, and, despite Dr. Prinz's warnings, he would most likely want to claim what was his soon if I didn't act. It wouldn't be an act of lovemaking. It would be revenge.

I had to leave. But where would I go and with whom? Just a few days ago, I'd thought it was with Jay. Now I didn't know. My thoughts became a muddle. I couldn't seem to imagine any scenario, any plan. It was as if I was holding my breath, waiting for something to happen that wouldn't require a decision from me.

Once again, I turned to Jordan for advice.

We met for a sail, and she was mightily impressed by my skill on the water.

"My dear, you'll be skippering a pirate schooner in the Caribbean, I suppose. Is that why you've been so interested in how to allocate your funds? Are you planning on securing a chest of gold doubloons to use in your new life?"

"Oh, I'd hoped I'd kept that secret. Did someone tell?" I laughed, the sun and wind restoring my spirits. "Now I'll need a new plan."

Once we anchored in a quiet bay and unwrapped sandwiches provided by Cook, I presented her my dilemma and my fears—that Jay was insufficiently connected to my daughter.

"Jay isn't opposed to having Pamela with us, but he's not enthusiastic," I complained.

"Not opposed—that's good news, isn't it?" she asked as we lolled on the aft section, picnic basket opened, Champagne poured, delights revealed.

"I have no intention of being an Anna Karenina," I bit out.

"I should hope not. What a grisly way to die—run over and chopped to pieces." She balled up her sandwich paper and tossed it into the basket. Leaning back, she closed her eyes and soaked up the sun. "You have to decide, darling. No one can do it for you. Do you want to stay with Tom or go with Jay? I can't tell you what to do. I wouldn't dare. Not now."

She *had* told me what to do, of course, when I'd received Jay's letter on my wedding eve, but that path was clearer. An unmarried pregnant woman did equal a ruined life. Jordan was a realist, and she accepted unchangeable facts, adjusting her attitude to accommodate them. I left out certain facts in my current dilemma.

I didn't tell her how I'd felt the afternoon I spoke to Jay about Pamela.

I didn't tell her about the associate of Anthony Delacorte who might be out to exact some revenge against Tom for his double-cross.

I didn't tell her that I now wondered if I should stay with either man or somehow chart a different course.

I didn't tell her any of these things because they troubled me so much, I could barely think. I had spent my life brushing aside unpleasant thoughts. It was a hard habit to break. Like Tom, I'd retreated to my comfortable position of avoiding any situation that required a show of courage. And that last possibility—charting a different course, all my own—took my breath away and stopped my thoughts. It was as frightening as being spirited away to a place like Mongolia, surrounded by primitives, not knowing their language.

After a while, Jordan closed her eyes as she relaxed against a pillow. "A woman has two choices in life," she said. "She can either marry into money. Or…she can live a terrible life without money."

I thought she was joking and started to politely laugh but, judging by her face, she was completely serious.

She went on: "Men can work for their money, can accumulate great piles of it. Women inherit it or work for it in other ways. Marriage is work."

Still lost in her reverie, she continued her sermon: "There are exceptions, but they are rare, and if you don't marry for money—I prefer to think of it as comfort—you must reconcile yourself to a very modest and possibly shabby life."

After a sigh, she said, "Men make their way in life, with or without a spouse. Women have no lives without a husband."

"Why, Jordan, you have no spouse, and you have a great life!" I protested.

She ignored my comment and at last opened her eyes and looked at me. "There is nothing wrong with choosing comfort, especially when adoring love comes as a bonus."

Was she talking of Jay or Tom? I suspected, deep down, that Tom still loved me. He thought of me, though, as a possession, something to be proud of, to show off. Did Jay think the same?

After a time, I hoisted the sails and directed us toward home, no more certain of what I wanted to do than when we'd left the dock.

Her little speech haunted me, though, as I pondered life without being beholden to Jay or Tom, without always having to be a supplicant of some kind, even in subtle ways. I just didn't know if I could live that shabby, "lonely" life she had talked about.

For a little while, I thought of nothing but enjoying the moment, and once again pushed unpleasant thoughts aside. It felt idyllic.

If I did anything at all to guard against bad outcomes, it was to manage my money. I cashed out of several big stock deals, I withdrew money from bank accounts, I sold jewelry. Yes, I worried about having such a large stash of actual greenbacks in my room, but I figured everything entailed risk, and I would rather have my treasure right there under my nose than a promise of more treasure to come.

As summer approached its last days, it treated us to a preview of fall. Blue skies, moderate temperatures, soft breezes with just the whisper of dying leaves from trees frazzled by the previous heat.

Tom went out of town, back to see his father on some family business. You would never know it from Nick's recounting of our story, but both of us did have surviving parents—he, his father, and me, my mother. I suppose it dimmed the romanticism of his telling, to see us with family still in our lives. Parentage made one real.

With Tom away, I worried about nothing. I rose, I swam—either on our little beach or in our pool. I played with Pammy. I spent afternoons with Jay.

It was a mark of my indecision that I never told Jay that Tom was away for a few days. I knew he would use that as a reason to pressure me into leaving at that moment. It was the perfect time to do so. Unsuspecting husband off in Chicago, Pamela and me alone. Jordan was gone, too, and Nick was particularly busy, so I didn't fear someone telling Jay about Tom's extended absence.

I just wanted what I wanted in that moment. Fears pushed aside. Suspicious husband gone. Lover content.

We didn't talk about the future anymore. We made a pact not to, to just live on the island of these moments together, and I devised a penalty for any time either of us used the words "tomorrow" or anything indicating a time beyond this one. The offender would have to rewind a clock to the previous hour, turning back time.

In just a few days, Jay's clocks were all running on different times, but we didn't care. We pretended they represented the times of countries we wanted to visit, so we'd attempt to speak the language of said country when entering that room. This usually devolved into hysterics as Jay had horrible mock accents. His German sounded Romanian, his French sounded Italian, and his Italian sounded like fishmongers in the Bronx.

Sometimes we swam together in his beautiful pool, and became tanned and blushed by the kiss of the sun.

I still had no idea what I wanted to do. Sometimes I thought that I'd just pack up everything, including Pamela, come to Jay's doorstep, and say, "Let's go away now."

Other times, I asked myself why I couldn't just continue as I was. Tom had mistresses and was likely to keep that habit as the years rolled by. Maybe he would have a litter of bastards by the time he was done. My anger over that dissipated as I worked on how to protect myself financially, so that my daughter would not be harmed by heirs showing up at any old moment to make a claim on her inheritance.

DAISY

With Nick's help, I had already managed to get Tom to agree to let me do my own stock buying with a small budget that I grew quickly. It was supposed to be a game, to see if I could choose good companies and make the money grow faster than Tom's similar investment pile.

I wasn't stupid enough to surpass him by much, though. I knew if I outwitted him by too large a margin, he'd stop the game in a fit of pique, then cut me off from it as well.

So I deferred to more modest selections, letting myself lose money occasionally, sometimes deliberately, sometimes because I wanted to see how a risk played out. But when I sensed some stocks were at a peak, I sold. I deposited the cash, then withdrew most of it. Nick helped me here, too, setting up a bank account for me—something separate from Tom's. Back then, a woman couldn't set up her own banking without a man.

My little stash of cash—in a secret drawer in my dresser—was in danger of spilling beyond its walls. Sometimes, I liked to lock the door and look at it, wondering if it was enough to push Pamela and me beyond just a shabby life and into a more comfortable one.

In fact, I began to dream that she and I would leave, and I'd have time to think, to decide whether to stay with Tom or go with Jay. Away from both of them, perhaps I could think more clearly.

Even though I tried to fail occasionally in my investments, I went through one particularly successful week, where I simply couldn't stop making good decisions. It seemed as if I had a sort of Midas touch, unable, even when I tried earnestly, to choose poorly. Unfortunately, this coincided with a time when Tom *was* doing particularly poorly, and, as usual, he didn't like being beaten, especially by his wife.

What was worse, he decided that our stock market game made for good dinner table conversation. Shortly after he returned from his trip to Chicago, we spent a miserable evening hosting Nick while Tom needled me about my luck and suggested I start betting on the horses next.

"You'll have to learn a thing or two about that, though," he said from his end of the table after taking a sip of wine. "It's not as simple as closing one's eyes and pointing to what you want."

"Don't insult Nick, dear," I said, tired of his teasing. "He's the one who does that blindfolded choosing, not me. You have a collection of them, don't you, Nick? Stylish blindfolds imported from Paris?"

Nick, who must have sensed the tension, happily followed my lead. "It's the best method. Written up in all the stocks and bonds articles I've been reading in the Yale Club library. Works between eighty and ninety percent of the time, and only the finest silk blindfolds will do."

Tom wasn't in a mood to be kidded, though. "Then why aren't you using that technique when advising me? I'm beginning to wonder if the two of you are plotting to make a fool out of me."

Nick had had too much to drink, so he injudiciously responded with more joking of his own. "Well, I suppose our plot is working then, isn't it, Daisy?" He smiled at me and winked, but I just gave him a stony stare, and he seemed to realize he'd gone too far, so he added, "Just kidding, Tom. I'll take a look at your portfolio first thing. Maybe we'll get you into some of the things Daisy's taken a shine to."

Instead of calming the waters, his reference to my choices just riled Tom more.

"I'm not taking investment advice from my wife. She can barely keep her household budget. When I married her, did you know she thought one could buy a car for, what was it, dear—five dollars?"

"I'd misread an advertisement," I said softly, my irritation spiking.

"And she buys so many things for Pamela—she bought her a diamond necklace the other day. The little dear will probably lose it if Daisy doesn't first. You lost that one I gave you, didn't you, dear?"

My face warmed. Yes, I had bought Pammy a necklace recently. Knowing its value, I thought it would be another good investment I might sell at some point, one that raised no suspicion. And, no, I hadn't lost my own similar piece of jewelry. I'd sold it and stored the money away. I had wanted to see how one did that—sell off one's jewelry—so I would know how to do it if I needed money. When Tom noticed I didn't wear it anymore, he'd asked about it and I had lied that I'd lost it.

"The chain was always flimsy," I said.

He laughed. "Good thing I manage the money. She and Pamela would be in rags if I didn't."

It was just before dusk, and the light outside was a warm yellow-gold. Tom's gaze turned to the windows and he stared across the Sound.

"I bet she thinks he" —Tom pointed to Jay's place—"has more money than I do. Not a chance. Not even close."

"How vulgar to talk about money at the dinner table," I said. In any event, I'd had enough. I stood. "I want some fresh air. I'm going to take a walk. Please, continue talking about money and how addle-brained I am on my own."

I left the room and hurried to the path that led to the promontory. It wasn't long, though, before I heard footsteps behind me and saw Nick running toward me, holding a wrap, obviously the excuse he'd used to leave the table and come after me.

"Daisy!" he called, handing me the cloth. "He's just a little drunk, that's all. Sorry if I made it worse."

I laughed bitterly. "You'd think he'd be proud of a wife able to do as well as I've been doing. He can't stand for anyone, especially a beautiful woman, to be better than him at something." Maybe that was Myrtle's charm, that she was so inferior to him in intellect and to me in beauty.

"He doesn't seem to mind Jordan being better at golf," he offered weakly.

I laughed again. "He doesn't care about golf."

"He cares about you."

I turned to him. "Then why does he have to destroy the things I love?" I continued walking toward the promontory, stopping when we got there. "Before marrying him, I loved to dance—and not just popular dances, either. I took ballet lessons. I was good at it. I painted. I was good at that, too. Then Tom said the dance lessons took too much time away from Pamela and him, and the painting made a mess the servants had trouble cleaning up."

He didn't say anything, and we just stood there, staring across the Sound to Jay's house, in shadows now except for a couple of lights on an upper floor. I imagined Jay sitting in his suite and reading, maybe glancing my way. How I wanted to be with him. At least with him I could laugh and joke and not worry about hiding my wit or tempering my intellect to suit his ego.

Looking down at the water, I remembered another thing I used to be good at. Diving. I loved the feeling of jumping into the air and hurtling head-first toward the deep end, feeling liberated for those few moments in the air, just myself and the air and the water. Nothing else.

Just then, I saw Tom approaching us. His grim, determined stride suggested he'd yank his silly little wife back to her prison and put her back on the shelf, where he could admire her.

Without thinking, I tore off my wrap and stepped forward; I had wanted to do this for so long. When I'd gone sailing, I'd looked up and calculated the dive on many a trip toward our dock.

"Daisy, no!" Nick cried, too late.

I threw myself into a perfect dive. I knew the water was deep here, and all I thought about was getting away on this perfect summer evening, becoming some kind of sea nymph who could frolic in the waves and eventually land on some perfect foreign shore.

For a few seconds, I felt it—liberation. Glorious, exultant freedom.

CHAPTER THIRTEEN

L ater, Nick told me that, after I dove, Tom raced to the promontory, ripped off his tie, and prepared to bolt into the water after me, but he couldn't bring himself to do it. He stood there, trembling with fear, Nick said, until he shouted that they needed to get the boat, and they hurried together to the pier.

By that time, I'd swum a good twenty feet out, but the current was strong, and, despite what my husband thought, I was no fool. Drowning in the Sound while my husband and cousin watched might have given me some pleasure, imagining their terror at the sight, but not enough to rip free of life itself.

I turned toward the pier just as Nick and Tom unmoored the boat and sailed my way. In a few minutes, I pulled myself over the side, dripping wet but feeling wonderful. Strong. Capable. Intelligent.

Unapologetic.

"I used to win prizes for my diving back in school," I said after Nick handed me his jacket. "And I've been wanting to make that dive ever since we moved here."

Tom said nothing, but he gave me a look combining sympathy with disgust, and I knew a visit from Dr. Prinz would likely be on the schedule the following day.

DAISY

Dr. Prinz did come by, but I managed to explain to him what a good athlete I was, how I loved swimming—something Tom could verify—that I had known the depth of the water and wasn't taking a risk when I dove. I even lied and said I'd made the dive before when no one was looking, and it was a wonderful form of exercise—good for both my mental health and physical health.

I don't know if he believed me, and he seemed a little frightened of me. Once he determined I was healthy and not in danger of harming myself, he packed up his bag as quickly as he could and left.

The stock market went back to punishing me as much as rewarding me, so Tom's envy abated. He talked of us moving again, maybe back to Chicago because he said his father seemed to be ailing, and he wanted to be closer to him.

"Chicago is so cold," I said one afternoon when I wished I could go over to Jay's. But Tom was staying in. He was doing that more and more, and I think it was deliberate, to keep a closer eye on me.

"New York is cold, too, at least in the winter." We both sat in the large parlor fronting the Sound, Tom with his latest book on the racial wars yet to come, me with a fashion magazine.

"Then we should head south," I said. "Florida. I've always wanted to see Florida."

He stared at me, and a malevolent sneer lifted up his lips. "Why, that's not a bad idea, dear. Just the two of us. We can leave Pammy with your mother, or Nanny. A second honeymoon."

My heart chilled. Tom's suggestion of leaving Pamela behind was an implicit threat. He was telling me he could direct our daughter away, whether I liked it or not.

I met his stare and said, as lightly as I could, "If we go to Florida, I would be absolutely horrible company without our daughter."

That ended that conversation.

For me, it was time for a final decision, and because Tom stayed close to home, I wasn't able to get over to see Jay for several days, and only then for a short visit, on the pretense of seeing Nick to discuss "family matters" that would bore Tom, I told him.

"We have to get away, darling," Jay told me, holding my hands as we sat in his study.

I'd told him how awful Tom had been to me, about diving, about how I wanted to get my life back somehow, all the things I'd loved to do before marrying.

"I can make it happen in an instant," he said. "You can paint, dance, swim, dive—all of it. I'd buy you a building full of studios, and install a diving board as high as you want for a thousand different pools!"

"I know." I looked down.

"Then let's stop waiting," he pleaded, kissing my hand. "Let's just leave."

"I have to do it when I can be sure I can take Pamela with me." I waited to hear if he'd object and was relieved when he didn't, though I would have preferred he endorse that position with vigor. I always seemed to be testing him on this lately.

"Europe or the South Seas? Which suits you?" he asked, his tone now jaunty. "Or would you rather stay in the States and go somewhere wild? Or we could go to Mexico. I know a great little town there with a villa we could rent. Sunshine and ocean views. Wonderful food. Music. You'll love it."

Again, I waited for him to add, "And Pamela, too. Pamela would not only love the weather, but she'll be brown as a berry by summer's end."

But he never said any such thing. Instead, he walked to the window, stared out, hands in his pockets, and planned our future. When I indicated mild interest in the Mexico plan, he described the villa in more detail. It wasn't as "grand" as "this place," but it had "charm" and lots of rooms, great "fixtures," and even a new garage that would accommodate three cars.

As he went on, I envisioned myself lolling about that mansion, and a great heaviness came over me as I realized I'd be trading one gilded cage for another. One job for another.

In my heart and mind, it was clearly time to leave Tom. What I couldn't quite bring myself to do was decide whether I needed to leave Jay, too. I wept inside at the prospect.

He had given me my old self back. He'd given me the best summer of my life. He'd given me hope and sparked in me little flashes of courage.

"Better hurry on over to Nick's," he said, staring out the window. "Tom's driving up."

There wasn't enough time to scurry over to Nick's. Besides, he wasn't there anyway. My visit to him had been a ruse.

Instead, Jay and I meandered out of his front door together, very casually, and then strolled over to Tom's car in front of Nick's cottage.

"Hello, old sport," Jay said jauntily.

"Nick wasn't here!" I cried, going to Tom. "He must have mixed up the time. Or maybe I did," I added, playing the fool.

"She stopped in to see if he was at my place," Jay said, smiling, and it felt as though we were supplying too many details.

Tom, still sitting in his coupe, looked at the car I'd driven here—a Ford that wasn't nearly as sporty. Thank God I had thought to leave it at Nick's and not at Jay's.

"How convenient," Tom said.

I leaned on his side of his car. "What brings you here?" I kept my tone light and sweet, as if it was the most natural thing in the world to talk to my husband in the presence of my lover, as if I was the most innocent woman in the world.

"Nick called," he said, "and when I said you were supposed to be visiting him, he seemed confused." His gaze flitted between us. "Said he must have forgotten and to offer his apologies."

Good old Nick, thinking quickly.

"I was just about to come back," I said.

"Hop in, darling," Tom now purred. "I'll have someone come retrieve the other car."

"Oh, that's silly, dear. I'll drive it back. I'll follow you," I said, starting to go for the Ford, but he reached out and grabbed my arm.

"No, I actually think it's silly for you to be here alone. Worse than silly, actually. Disrespectful."

His last word hung in the air, and it was clear he was claiming his property—me.

Jay took a step forward as if he was going to brawl, but I held up my hand.

"Tom's right. I should be going." I looked at Jay and mentally pleaded with him not to roil the waters. "Thank you for keeping me company while we waited for Nick to show up."

Still, Jay came toward me and opened the passenger door, and I'd barely made myself comfortable before Tom roared us away.

I couldn't get to Jay over the next few days. Tom stayed around the house all the time now. He even insisted on spending time with me. We went sailing one day, swimming the next, and I couldn't shake the feeling that he had figured something out and needed to decide how to deal with it. He was just looking for more clues to solidify his case, like some zealous prosecutor getting ready to go to court.

This made me even more anxious to leave, afraid of what his ultimate plan would be—confrontation? I didn't know what I would say. I practiced denials and confessions that I discarded. No, I had not betrayed him. How could he think that? Or, yes, I had enjoyed time with Jay, but how could he blame me when he himself was not blameless? It all felt weak and thin.

If Tom did accuse me, it wouldn't end well. Admitting his wife was unfaithful would be a blow for him to absorb, and I knew he'd fight back in some way, even physically.

This forced me back to thinking of running away with Jay. He would know how to get us some place safe where Tom couldn't find us. I wasn't confident enough to do that on my own. Not yet, at least.

I felt my daydream of a summer had turned into a nightmare, and I slept fitfully, woke scared, and felt uncertain. All that newfound confidence disappeared.

Now I was committed to retreating to Mexico with Jay, if only to get away from Tom. After that, I didn't know. But it was the first step. I merely had to let Jay know the when and where.

But how could anyone think at all of anything? Summer decided to hurl one last burst of awful heat at us at the end of the month, as if to say "see what happens when you wish me gone—I'll show you."

When you opened the door, all you felt was an oven-like blast and no breeze. There was no sailing now, and no swimming either as the skies promised lightning each afternoon, taunting us before cruelly holding back rain.

The day was all about waiting for the night, knowing that even its darkness would offer sweaty sheets and damp pillows.

I awoke one of those mornings, sighed, and planned to do nothing but look for escapes of the more immediate kind. A swim. A cool bath. Another bath perhaps.

I thought of penning a note to Jay, telling him to let me know when he wanted to leave, but I was too afraid it would be intercepted. I didn't know if I could trust any of our household staff. I kept Pammy near me a lot, so much so that the nanny even complained that it was better for the child if I didn't interfere with her regimen.

Tom was suspicious of me, and I was growing suspicious of everyone else.

I had to get away. I was even at the point where I calculated how much time I would need to pack up our things and get over to Jay's. I thought I could do it all within twenty minutes. Was that enough time to elude Tom's clutches? What if Jay wasn't there when I arrived? Then what?

That night at dinner, Tom pointed out that Gatsby had shut down his parties, and word in town was he'd hired new staff so no one would gossip about a lover he'd taken.

There was a long pause as he looked at me across the table.

Oh, I didn't stir a bit. I didn't blink. I couldn't give him any hint of embarrassment or fear, even though it curdled my stomach.

"Well, it's nice not to have all that tomfoolery going on in our backyard, don't you think, dear?" I said. And please, pass me the roast. "Maybe he's gone out of town."

I desperately wanted to know if Jay was there. I was hoping for information, for Tom to say, oh, no, the man was still over there, he'd seen him. Then I'd know I could drive over in the morning, maybe even tonight.

The next day, however, he did give me some more information about Jay. Or rather, he told me he had decided to invite Jay to lunch, along with Nick and Jordan, to talk over some business opportunities, he said. I sensed another purpose—perhaps an examination of my interaction with Jay, a sleuthing for clues about our relationship, or even some public humiliation of me. The blistering heat pulled good sense and reason from me, and I couldn't think of a way to avoid this encounter. At least I would see Jay, and maybe there would be a private moment when we could plot our departure.

Other than diving into the Sound again and swimming over to Jay's pier, I couldn't conjure up another plan. So I resolved to just get through it, to become the porcelain figure bending toward her rugged cavalier, wait for the heat to end and cool reasoning to return, and then put the final touches on my escape plan.

Yet, like an oracle of old, I sensed it coming—disaster.

CHAPTER FOURTEEN

J ay arrived just before noon the next day, and we all sat on the dim veranda having drinks. Though the curtains were drawn to keep out the sun, sweat coated Tom's face, which I knew made him self-conscious. Nanny brought Pammy in to say hello, and she ran to Jay as if she thought he was some beloved uncle. Nick and Jordan tried too hard to be funny.

I was the perfect housewife and hostess, sweetly attentive to Tom, so if this was some kind of test, some sort of gathering of clues, Tom would find nothing but bright, shining innocence.

I tried, at one point, to head outside alone, hoping Jay would follow so we could talk. I said I thought the sailboat's ropes looked loose and would go check them, but Tom called a servant and had him do it instead. Pointedly, he remarked while looking only at me that he had been instructing our servants to regularly "keep an eye" on the boat. I felt the walls closing in.

We had finished our second round of drinks, and now I thought perhaps we would end the afternoon with a light lunch and goodbyes—maybe goodbyes that would let me talk to Jay at the car alone. Perhaps it would all be over with Tom deciding he was too afraid to ignite a confrontation, when someone—was it Jordan?—suggested driving into the city. It was a quiet afternoon; the drive would at least provide us some cooling air. At least, that was the argument.

I said I was too tired and it was too hot to think of moving even a finger, but somehow this became the plan everyone enthusiastically endorsed, and my misgivings were overruled. Tom in particular thought it a great idea, but he might have thought it was good to punish me this way by forcing me out into the scouring heat when he knew I didn't want to go. I noted this and decided to choose the things I didn't want, knowing he'd push for the opposite.

My mind might have been addled by the heat and drink and apprehension, but I knew how to manage Tom. I wanted it all to be over and I wanted to sink into my bed, sleep, and wait for fall's cooling temperatures to bathe us, and somehow for a path to be lit for me. So far, he had not caused a row, and I suspected this day was some kind of punishment for me that would be followed by stern warnings in private and ever more vigilant servants watching all my moves.

We were soon on the gravel drive, and Tom suggested I take our coupe since he knew I loved to drive, which was true, though not in this burning weather. Using my new strategy, I was about to say that would be delightful, figuring he would then change the plan, when Jay interceded and insisted Tom give Jay's gleaming yellow roadster a go.

Before Tom could object, Jay was in the driver's seat of the coupe with me as passenger, and Tom was behind the wheel of the "circus car," as he dubbed it, with Nick and Jordan in tow.

"Thank you," I said as we took off. "I didn't want to drive."

"I could tell," he said, and smiled at me. "Let's have a few drinks in town and get this over with."

"Yes!" I agreed with passion, though I still wasn't clear what Tom planned for this day. "I couldn't wait to talk to you," I gushed. "I've been a prisoner. It's been awful." At last we could speak freely.

"Oh, darling," he said and grabbed my hand for a quick kiss before shifting gears.

"I think Tom knows," I said. The car stirred up a breeze, but it was a warm one, and it did little to cool our brows.

He nodded. "I hope he does!"

"No, don't say that," I answered. "It's better if he doesn't, or at least doesn't admit it. If we can just keep him in the dark a little longer, it will be for the best." I wanted no confrontations, no fights. I just wanted to safely get away with Pammy. To that, Tom presented the greatest threat. Later, I would deal with my feelings for Jay and what to do about being with him or not.

"How long? To keep him in the dark? Shouldn't we go as soon as possible now?" Jay asked as he smoothly shifted gears again.

"Yes, yes. As soon as possible," I said. "Tonight, he'd be suspicious. Maybe tomorrow. Or the next day. I just need to be sure I can take my daughter with me without Tom knowing."

Finally being able to talk with Jay about these plans calmed me. At last, I was choosing something, at least for the time being. I'd run away with Jay and then decide next steps, if any.

"You'll be patient, won't you, darling?" I needed to find a time when Tom wouldn't be suspicious if I took Pammy somewhere alone.

Lately, if I'd even hinted at such an expedition, he'd immediately say he would accompany us.

"I'll try," Jay said.

"I think it might be best at night," I said, "but I don't want Pammy crying and waking up Tom."

"Tomorrow night?" he asked. "The sooner, the better. I'm ready. We can fly somewhere. Have you been in an airplane?"

"Yes, but Pammy hasn't."

"She'll love it," he said, his confidence bringing me additional calmness. And the fact that he had thought of her enjoyment buoyed me.

"If we don't make it tomorrow night, the night after," I said.

"I'll wait for you. If it takes a hundred days, I'll wait," he affirmed.

With our vague plan decided on, off we went, into town, past the ash heaps that made me shudder, over the bridge that provided a cooling view, with Tom behind us as if he were a police agent on the tail of an ignominious bootlegger.

Once in the city, we slowed, and those warm winds ended. The heat descended again in full force, wrapping us all in a heavy blanket, unmitigated by the shade cast by skyscrapers. At an intersection, Nick hurried forward to tell us the plan was to head to the Plaza, where we would get a room and cool drinks. We'd wait out the worst of the heat before heading back to the Sound.

Jay looked at me, his eyebrows raised, as if to say, "See, I told you. A few drinks and we'll be done," and we drove to the hotel.

No drink was cool on the tenth floor, however. My god, the heat here was even more oppressive. We opened windows, every single one of them, from the sitting room to the bathroom to the bedroom of the suite, but nothing helped.

I sat on a couch fanning myself with a room service menu while Nick or Tom or Jordan called for ice and whiskey. I was just waiting for the day to be over.

The drinks were delivered, and Jay and Tom both rushed to pay and tip the room service fellow, with Jay winning the honor. Tom stepped back, smiled, and said, "Go ahead, spend your money on my drinks. I'm happy to oblige."

We toasted the end of summer.

And then…it began, everything I had feared. Here I'd thought I had escaped the worst, that all that remained was maybe an hour in this cell of a suite, and we would be back to cooler skies and a cooler home.

Tom began needling Jay, first about his money, then about his education, then about flirting with me. They stood behind the couch, and Tom's sweat dripped on me when he spoke.

I cringed, hoping Jay would stay good-natured since this torturous day was so close to being over. We were so close to our escape—my escape.

He did show restraint. At first.

Jay answered each mocking comment with good cheer, and when it came to me, well, he must have decided honesty was the best strategy.

"Your wife is beautiful and charming, old sport," he said, smiling, the faintest veneer of sweat on his brow. "Who wouldn't want to flirt with her?"

"Gentlemen, that's who," Tom spit out. "Which, it seems, you are not, *old sport.*"

Nick attempted a joke from his position by an open window.

"Gentlemen are no longer in style, Tom. I read it in the *Times* just this week, didn't you know? Gigolos and scoundrels are all the rage."

It fell flat.

Then Jay said, seriously, "I'm a gentleman who treats a woman the way she should be treated." He looked at me. "And if she decided she preferred another approach, I'd happily accept the outcome."

I thought Tom might swing at Jay then. He loosened his tie and took off his jacket, but Nick interceded, walking over to the two, putting his drink down as if he meant business.

"I can't speak for myself, but we're all gentlemen here," he said, still trying to amuse. "Except for the doorman, perhaps. He looked like a rake to me."

Jordan huffed out her frustration with his efforts and stepped forward from her window perch, as well.

"I officially declare the war over and peace treaties to be signed forthwith," she pronounced, holding up her glass in a toast.

"Hear, hear!" Nick added.

For a moment, this interlude seemed to work, but then Tom beckoned me. "Come here," he said, and when I didn't move, he repeated it, more forcefully. "Come here!"

I felt obliged to respond, if only to keep the truce, knowing resistance would make him bolder. I stood and walked round to him and sighed. I felt like a prisoner being led to execution.

"Tell him you do not like him flirting with you." He grabbed my elbow and turned me to face Jay. "Tell him you want him to stop. Tell. Him."

The room buzzed with silence and heat and a claustrophobic tension.

Somewhere below, a wedding was going on, and the music and cheers reached us on such a still day. How awful, to be married in this heat.

I said nothing. I couldn't think of anything that would make things better, and I had no intention of making them worse. If I did what he said, he'd press for more. If I refused, he'd most likely fight Jay right there in that hideously warm room.

"Oh, Tom," I uttered at last, as if he were a disobedient imp. "Don't be silly. All women love to be flirted with."

That just stirred Jay, though, and he leapt to what he must have thought was my defense. Our defense.

"Tell him the truth, darling," Jay said. "Tell him you want to leave him," he said in a low, serious voice, as if he was tired of pretending this was fun.

Oh, no. I'd figured on Tom's recklessness, not on Jay's. I thought Jay understood; this wasn't the time to provoke Tom. I had told him not to and he'd disregarded my warning. I'd told him to be careful! To be patient!

Who could be patient in this heat? It lit up nerve endings, crackling electricity along every fiber.

But I wouldn't err again, so I remained mute.

Nick, from back in a corner again, said, "Come on, now. Let's stop this. We've all had too much to drink, and the heat's making us crazy. Let's go home." A feeble effort from a feeble man.

"Are you his lover?" Tom blurted out.

Whiskey loosened my tongue. "Lover? Ha! You're concerned about lovers? Do you have one, Tom? A lover? Perhaps a pregnant one? That conniving witch Myrtle Wilson?"

He raised his hand and slapped me, the movement so sudden, the pain so sharp that, none of us registered it for a few seconds and then, I bent over, holding my cheek, crying.

"How dare you, you bastard? How dare you? You're as common as your cheap whore," I spat out as Jay stepped forward, ready to return Tom's blow, but Nick sped into action and pulled Jay back. "Calm down now," he said. "No need for this."

Jordan also stepped up. "I think it's time to go," she said, coming over to me, putting her arm around my shoulders. She looked at Tom. "Gentlemen don't hit ladies," she seethed, her voice shaking with fury.

She started to lead me toward the door, but Jay objected. Reaching out to me, he pulled me under his protective embrace.

"No, they don't," he said. "Gentlemen fight fair. When they fight at all." That was a blow aimed at Tom's manhood, at his lack of war service, and I waited for more violence.

But between Jordan's judgment and Jay's well-placed verbal blow, Tom seemed confused, unsure what to do next. He clenched and unclenched his hands at his sides.

Emboldened, Jay went on, his grip around my shoulders tighter. "She loves me. She wants to be with me."

When I didn't immediately concur, he looked at me. "You do love me, right?"

Whimpering from my still stinging cheek, I nodded.

"You're going to leave Tom, right?" His voice sounded higher than usual.

"I...I..." I couldn't speak, and the room seemed to spin. I must have swooned, because the next thing I knew, I was lying on the bed in the room next to the parlor and Jay was pressing a cool cloth to my head and whispering something to me. I couldn't focus on it at first, but eventually the words made sense.

"He'll be out of the picture soon. Remember, I've spoken to Anthony. Don't worry. He's not going to do anything while you're around. You don't need to be afraid."

Ah, yes, the gangster. I had pushed that out of my mind and, when nothing bad happened, I figured it never would.

Then Tom came in and pushed Jay away, grabbed the wet cloth, and threw it on the floor.

"We're leaving!" he announced. I recognized that take-charge tone, and I knew I should obey.

"Not if you want to go in one piece," Jay said, barely glancing at him.

Nick stood in the doorway next to Tom. "Let's all go. Come on. All of us."

Jordan brushed past them both and came over to me.

"Yes, let's." She helped me up.

Somehow, I managed to find the strength and wherewithal to stand. With purpose, I shook off her hand and strode to the door, both Nick and Tom stepping out of my way, parting like some sea pulled by an invisible hand. I gathered my hat and bag.

I had one thought in mind at that moment—getting safely home to Pamela. I'd leave Tom within seconds after that if I could make it away, but first I needed to get to her. Tom would never let me be alone with her again, now that he knew of my infidelity.

"I need to go home. To rest. We'll all…see each other tomorrow." I looked at Jay. I tried to convey the thought through my eyes: "Not now, love. Not now."

I don't know if he received the message because Tom came my way and enthusiastically agreed with my plan.

"I'll get you home, dear," he said.

Jay stepped forward to object, but I stopped him. "Let me go now," I said. "I need to get to my daughter."

He understood and stopped.

I said to Tom, "I'll drive. I've had less than you to drink."

What you have to understand is that Nick didn't know who was behind the wheel that night. He had assumed it was me because of what I said before leaving, and in his muddled memory, he also seemed to think it was Jay I left with, not Tom, maybe because he was a hopeless romantic and wanted to see us together in the end. We'd driven into the city together, after all. Or maybe it was because Nick was drunk and his grasp of events hazy.

But Tom would never have let me leave that room with Jay. He would have thrown us both out the window before allowing that humiliation. He'd already been bested by Jay in the room. I'm sure Jay's remark about men choosing to fight rang in his ears. He'd been on our bumper practically the whole way to the city, too, probably scared we were going to run off then and there. Why on earth would he acquiesce to my lover driving me home when a short hour before he'd been afraid Jay and I would just drive off somewhere together, lost to him forever?

So it was Tom and me in the car, and, no, it wasn't me behind the wheel.

On the street outside the Plaza, Tom grabbed me, hard and fast around the waist, and I struggled to break free. When I did and managed a few quick strides up the street, he caught up quickly enough, found my hand, and yanked me forward. We were now in front of Jay's bright circus machine.

"Get in!" he shouted, embarrassing me in front of the doorman. "Let him drive my old coupe back." And he laughed, probably thinking of the three of them squeezed into that small seat.

I thought of running again, but the only thing binding me to Tom now was Pammy, and I wouldn't let him reach home first so he could place her somewhere out of my reach. I was stone cold sober at that point and thinking fast. He knew Jay and I were lovers. He feared we would run away together. He would do anything to prevent that, including holding our daughter hostage so I, his prized possession, would return to him.

"Let me drive," I said, but he came round to the passenger side, opened the door, and shoved me down into the car. With a leap that almost caused him to tumble, he jumped into the driver's seat and tried starting the engine. But Jay had one of those newfangled keys needed before the starter button would work, and Tom cursed, obviously remembering. He soon found the key in his pocket.

All I could think of then was my daughter, getting home to her, making sure she was safe and …mine. I started mapping out my plan as Tom drove, not paying attention to his weaving and speeding as dusk settled over the city.

I would sleep in Pamela's room that night, I decided. I'd pack our bags quietly while Tom slept off his drinks. Maybe I would take off in the dead of night while Tom dozed.

Take off to Jay's? He'd be there, waiting for me, I knew, despite our plan to leave the next night.

Would we head for Mexico?

If so, I'd be going from one cage to another. And how safe would that new cage be? Jay knew bad men who could do bad things. I wondered what he would do to me if I ever wanted to leave him, as I was leaving Tom. Would he become as malevolent as Tom was now? He had spent years looking for me already. He could do it again, probably more successfully than Tom.

These thoughts and more tumbled through my mind as the wind blew my hair round my head. I didn't bother securing it with my hat or a scarf. I didn't care. I just wanted to get home. Tom was pressing the vehicle into shudderingly high speeds. I think he wanted to wreck that car, and us in it, and so, as we approached that ash heap section of the drive that I hated so much, I turned to him and said, "Slow down or you'll make me sick."

He glanced at me for a long moment. Too long.

Suddenly, something whacked the car with a loud thump. At first, I thought a tire had blown, but somehow we were still moving, and Tom was swerving so fast that I fell against him.

DAISY

"For god's sake, Tom!" I cried, now pushing the hair out of my face so I could see. But the lights of the roadster showed only grim roadway ahead. I turned around and saw another car that had just passed us jolting over a big bump of something—perhaps the same obstacle we had encountered, and thought nothing of it.

I thought instead of getting home and safe to my daughter.

CHAPTER FIFTEEN

By now, you know what happened after that awful day, and that horrible drive home. Tom hadn't hit just any obstacle. He'd crashed into his mistress, who had run out into the street fleeing her husband. Flung to the ground, she'd been crushed by a vehicle headed the other way. It was a gruesome death—one I wouldn't wish on an enemy—and I took no pleasure in reading and hearing of it over the next days.

At home that night, I hurried up to Pammy's room, locked the door, and lay down on the small bed reserved for Nanny when the little girl couldn't sleep.

Tom yelled through the door. "Don't think I'll let you go! He's a social climber. He's nothing! He's not like you and me, Daisy! Nothing like us!"

I couldn't resist, got up, and shouted back, "Thank God!"

Then I heard an engine start up and looked out the window. Our poor butler and housekeeper—Tom must have roused them—drove each of our vehicles somewhere away from our house. He was cutting off my means of escape.

There was nothing I could do. I lay down again and tried to sleep.

DAISY

The next morning, I concentrated on just keeping the peace. I'd stay quiet and agreeable, not speaking of the afternoon at the Plaza or even the bruise on my cheek.

But somehow, the papers had gotten hold of the accident before going to press the night before, and Tom, his hands shaking so hard he couldn't hold the pages upright, read that he'd killed his mistress. It was just one paragraph, probably hastily written to make the paper's deadline, merely the who, what, where, and when of Myrtle's death under the headline: "Garage Owner's Wife Killed."

He said nothing. He got up and walked to the windows. He looked out at the Sound. Then he practically ran to the garage.

Although he'd moved our own cars off property, he had yet to return Jay's car, knowing I couldn't start it without the key, so he hurried and made arrangements for it to be driven over to Jay's mansion. He seemed to calm down after that was taken care of, with the murder weapon placed far enough away to keep his hands clean, and his innocence secure.

I had no doubt that, if questioned, he would say he drove his own car home that night and didn't know who drove Jay's. If pressed with conflicting stories, he would probably laugh and admit we were all drunk, and everyone else must have been confused because he had driven the roadster into town, but it's a circus car and one ride in it was enough for him.

I could hear it in my head, those easy lies. Police would believe him. They believed the Toms of the world.

Now, as sunshine streamed through the windows, he came back into the room, hands in his pockets, and walked to the doors.

"We're moving," he announced after a time. "Back to Chicago. I've been making the arrangements, as you know, and I'm speeding them up."

I could sense his fear that the accident would be traced to him, and he'd be held responsible, despite it being Jay's car, delivered to Jay's garage, despite any easy alibis he could conjure up.

So this became part of my plan, to use his fear, and I managed to call Nick later that day, simply instructing him to tell Jay to be patient.

That night, after I fed Pammy, bathed her, and tucked her into bed, we sat in the kitchen and supped on cold chicken and beer. Tom had sent the staff home after taking care of Jay's car, finalizing the arrangements with movers, and securing us a house to rent along the lake in Chicago. I said what we both knew:

"You killed her." I wiped my face with my napkin. "We hit her. You were driving."

He swallowed and stared at me, and for one terrible moment, I feared Tom, that he might decide to get rid of this annoying witness to his crime. He stood and strode out of the room to the parlor, where he grabbed a bottle of whiskey and poured himself a tall glass. I followed and stood by the door.

"It's all right, Tom. I'm your wife. I can't and won't betray you. It's our little secret." As long as he treated me right, as long as he let me do what I wanted, even taking Pammy on an excursion without him.

185

He poured and downed another drink, then his head dropped to his chest and he let out an animal-like cry, so anguished that I thought he was having some kind of attack.

I didn't go to him, though. I let him ponder his fate alone, and, shaken, I eventually sank into an embroidered chair, still close to the door should I want to flee.

He turned and came to me. He knelt in front of me and slurred words of contrition and gratitude.

"I didn't see her. I swear I didn't see her," he cried. "It wasn't my fault. She ran into the road. It was dark. I didn't see her! Oh, Daisy, Daisy. I knew I could count on you."

He wept. He sobbed into my lap like a little boy who longed for his parents' affection after engaging in some particularly devious mischief. He begged my forgiveness. He promised me everything.

In those moments when he was at my feet and I was stroking his hair, I remembered falling in love with him—prizing both his strength and his vulnerability. I'd seen it when we were younger. It had been the same as mine. The same longing for the world to be kind, not cruel, the same yearning for people to understand and accommodate you, not to judge you.

He'd been stuck, just like me, in a time and place, and he, too, was afraid of being less than the best. The best football star. The best polo player. The best son. The best representative of his class and culture.

He tried so hard.

I remembered him on the altar at our wedding, his face freshly scrubbed, his brown eyes shining with confusion.

I remembered my heart about to burst with love for him on our honeymoon, once I had determined that was my fate.

And I remembered our wedding night, when he was tender, sweet, and gentle, treating me as if I were that bit of porcelain that might break.

How could I not soothe him?

So I did, gently shushing him, telling him things would be all right, that we'd go away, and not look back, that everything would be different.

I lied.

Even in these tender moments of remembrance, I knew he couldn't be different. I barely had it within me to change, but somehow I had to find the grit to do so.

I knew he would eventually secure another mistress, and it wouldn't be long before she'd show up with a bastard, and he would be harsher on me now that he had tasted the thrill of roughing me up, as he had Myrtle.

If he had one ability to change, it seemed to be to shed the finer qualities of manhood that his social status had required of him. In these freewheeling years, he was learning he didn't need to abide by any rules, even self-imposed ones.

DAISY

He had accidentally killed his mistress, a troublesome woman. It wouldn't be long before he lost his remorse and realized how convenient that solution was. I didn't intend to be his next victim.

So I comforted him as best I could, led him to bed, and sneaked back to my own, ever more eager to leave. I was almost ready, but with my leverage over Tom, I could afford to do more. I had some more jewelry I wanted to sell off, and I thought I could do it in at most a day or two, while I finished the details of my plan. I tried ringing up Nick to urge him to tell Jay one more time to be patient, but Nick wasn't home.

In the morning, we awoke to more news. Mr. Wilson had exacted his revenge, finding and killing the owner of the car that had run down his wife.

CHAPTER SIXTEEN

I heard the news from Tom, who reported it coldly over coffee.

"Cook tells me there was a disturbance across the way yesterday. That Wilson fellow tracked down his wife's killer and shot him."

I gripped my coffee cup. I stopped breathing. For an instant, a wild hope emerged, that Wilson had shot a servant. But Jay had sent the servants away.

In that instant, I knew my lover was dead, and I no longer had leverage over Tom.

"Wh-what…" I murmured and then stilled as the news hit home.

I had loved Jay, loved him with all the pure, sweet affection of one's first attachment. To leave him, to betray him, was to betray oneself. And that was why I'd been so tortured all those years until reuniting. I'd thought I had cheated myself, not just Jay, upon marrying Tom. I had given up trying to be good and kind and tender. I'd thought one couldn't be that way and survive.

I wanted to ask for more details but couldn't. I choked on the words. I blinked fast to avoid tears. I stared at Tom, daring him to say more, knowing he would because it would hurt me. How cold he was.

"Just marched in to the house, found him in the pool, and fired his pistol. Good aim, apparently." Tom smirked. "They'll have to drain the pool now, of course."

Of course. I put down my napkin, stood, and walked silently up to my room, where I closed the door and sat on the bed, trembling.

Tears came, then sobs that I didn't bother hiding. Let Tom hear. Let him hear how much I loved Jay. I moaned and wailed. I got up and paced. I cursed. I wanted the world to witness my anguish.

Loathsome Tom, giving me the news with such glee. I'm sure he now believed in his heart that Jay had been Myrtle's killer, after all. In a short time, he would erase all doubt and remember it this way, that Jay had run over his mistress. For all I know, Tom might have later told Nick that I was behind the wheel that night, thus triggering his version of the tale.

My heart was again broken, that again the world of sunshine and love and beauty and tenderness had drifted out of reach. The world and life had again disappointed me.

I, like Jay, had lived in a fairyland before the war. Peaceful, hopeful, loving, gentle. Those years, our youthful years, were everything you'd wanted as you stepped into the world. And then…destruction on a level unimaginable. Illness scouring the land as if an avenging angel had come to punish all of us for the folly of the war.

Everything changed after those years of rupture, and he'd spent such a long time searching, searching for me, trying to get it all back. Seduced by Jay's fantasy, I, like him, thought we both could reclaim our pre-war happiness because I wanted the same thing. But I didn't know how to turn back the clock, to go back in time and recapture everything we had lost—that Eden in which we'd grown up.

There was no going back, only moving forward. Jay, of all people, should have known that, he with his aspirations for success, his drive always toward the horizon.

The phone rang. It was Nick. I heard Tom tell him I was indisposed. It rang again. Jordan this time—she'd stayed in the city rather than squeeze into the coupe with Jay and Nick that awful night after the afternoon at the Plaza. Tom gave the same excuse to her. I wasn't feeling well, couldn't come to the phone.

His steely voice told me I had to get away and soon. No more waiting to sell jewelry or finalize plans. Panicked and grief-stricken, I had to find the courage and wits to get out from under his control. With Pammy. No one could make this plan for me. I had to do it myself.

It didn't matter that I couldn't speak to Nick or Jordan. After all, what would I say? Tom was carefully watching me, so I couldn't afford to make him angry. If I did, my future would include a visit or two from Dr. Prinz with his long syringe. Then I'd be lucky to see Pammy when she visited me in an asylum.

My mind and heart were tumbling, my thoughts and feelings a knotted ball I couldn't pull apart. I just put one foot in front of the other that day and during the hours to come. Of Tom's moving plans, I nodded approval. I helped Nanny pack Pamela's things. I boxed up some of my items. All these actions were parallel to my own planning. As my fogged mind cleared, I knew what I had to do and plotted the best time to do it.

DAISY

Jay's death felt like a constant ache, like a bruise that wouldn't heal. The irony of his loss was that, sometime on the road back home from the city that dreadful night, I'd been coming to the conclusion that I couldn't be with him, not for any length of time, at least. The real reason I'd not immediately fled to his mansion with Pamela was my hesitation at being imprisoned in yet another gilded cell. The real reason I had continued to send messages for him to be patient was that I wasn't sure I would ever show up.

Even with those realizations, I never wanted his life snuffed out. Certainly not like this. His life was taken in such a despicable way, killed by a garage owner from that ash heap part of town, and not in some grand heroic way that would have immortalized him in an appropriate fashion.

Now that he was gone, though, I could chart a course free of worrying that he'd come looking for me again. To realize this benefit of his passing only added to my grief.

I'm ashamed to admit it, but eventually, maybe sooner than was seemly, I even felt some relief, knowing I wouldn't have to run away from two men, one of whom had already spent years tracking me down and could possibly do so again.

Nick later reported to me the pathetic gathering at Jay's funeral. Just Nick and a few others. He had attracted hundreds to his parties, and many felt left out if they'd not attended one.

Jay had created a dream life for himself, and it turns out all his friends were imaginary, too.

I couldn't spend too much time thinking of these things, though later I pondered them at length, wondering if I really had been a fairy that summer. Sometimes, I cried at the thought of Jay dying alone, and with so few to mourn him.

At that moment, I had problems I needed to face—Tom. During those days of planning to move, he had a look in his eye that sent shivers down my spine. Cold. Evaluating. Waiting for the moment we were in a new home, with no one around to watch out for me, to protect me from his slowly simmering anger. He would make me pay for my infidelity.

I had to give it one last look before we left, and in the early morning hours two days later, I stole out of my bed, tied a scarf around my neck, and drove to West Egg without Tom's knowledge. He'd felt comfortable enough with my new agreeable nature that the cars were back on our property again. I had presented nothing but the most obedient of temperaments to him, talking of our new home in Chicago, asking how many rooms it had, if I could hire a decorator. He thought I was his old Daisy again, the one who did what was expected of her, the one who was careless and thoughtless in the face of others' misfortunes.

Dawn broke and the light painted Jay's mansion golden, but it stood silent and empty, its master now gone for good, and for a moment it seemed to be rebuking me, mutely asking why I'd not visited earlier, why I hadn't saved its owner. I wondered that, too.

Who would be the next Gatsby, the next man to conjure up a past at Oxford or some other elite school and make a fortune that allowed him to dazzle and charm and have his way with everyone?

As I walked the grounds, I remembered the better side of him, the eager, striving side that approached the world with an openness usually demonstrated only by naïfs. I loved that about him. I wouldn't deny it.

Making my way back to my car, I saw a dark vehicle approach and a man get out, someone I recognized as a Delacorte associate.

With a breezy hello, I introduced myself, using my maiden name, and said I thought I knew him.

"It's a shame, real shame what happened to Jay," he said, shaking his head. "A good man. One of the best I ever knew."

"Yes, yes," I said. "I was a friend. I'll…I'll miss him." On that last word, my voice cracked, and I began to cry.

"There, there, Miss," he said. He came over to me and handed me a handkerchief, while I continued to weep.

It was a genuine cry, and I realized it felt good to share this grief with someone, not just in private or in whispered conversations with Nick, because I knew Tom would take offense at any outpouring of sorrow for Jay Gatsby.

The man tried to comfort me, patting me on the back, saying "there, there" over and over.

Finally, I gathered my wits and sniffed, standing straight.

"So much was left hanging after his death," I said. "I don't know what to do."

"Oh, that's right, Miss. That's right. I was hoping to get some counsel myself, about a matter I'm supposed to take care of."

I knew what he was talking about. The matter with Tom.

I paused. I knew I could just leave and say nothing. In those endless seconds, Tom's life and death teetered.

"If Jay wanted something done, I would think he'd want it done. Even post mortem."

I played the part of the fool, the empty-headed woman who leaves business matters to the men.

"Yes, ma'am," he said after some hesitation. "You're probably right."

After a few more moments of empty small talk, we parted ways.

After hurrying home, I found the house to be a jumble of activity, movers lifting and carrying out furniture, servants packing, little Pammy running to and fro with Nanny at her heels. I secured her suitcase and my own, filled with dresses and outfits and makeup and perfume. And money, too. One should always have abundant cash on hand.

I smiled and frowned at all the right moments, playing my role as attentive wife and mother, all the while hurrying as fast as I could, not wanting to be around if Mr. Delacorte's associate decided to fulfill the contract then and there.

Things were a blur, and I was frazzled. It was warm, but the effervescence of the season had long since gone, and we all were stumbling into that season of farewells—fall.

Tom trod out to the car and hoisted a box into the back seat. Turning to me, he smiled and said, "Anything else?"

"Just a few things for the car," I answered and handed him a hatbox and a small piece of luggage for overnight visits stuffed with things I didn't need. It was such an awkward size and shape, it took him some time to secure it. "Stay here while I get them," I said.

I gave him a quick peck on the cheek, feeling his stubble, remembering how his manliness used to thrill me, but he didn't respond. He stayed busy tying down items.

One last glance, and I was off, flitting as fast as that fairy I'd imagined glowing in our dock light.

The house reverberated with a quiet hum of activity—thumps of furniture, clicks of doors, murmured voices.

I ran to the nursery. I gathered my two large suitcases, one in each hand, and I told Nanny that Pamela would be in my charge now. I'd thought of stowing our luggage on the boat earlier, but had been afraid some servant would find it, since we would be getting ready to sell the boat soon, and Tom might have instructed some worker to get it in tip-top shape. Quietly, I led my daughter down the back stairs and out to the lawn, where we walked as if it was all part of our moving plan, to the boat.

My nerves jangled with apprehension. I had planned this. I'd known this was my only chance, when movers filled the house, when Tom trusted me to help with directions, even keeping Pammy out of the way. I had to act fast before he wanted something from me or noticed I wasn't to be found.

"Here, darling," I said as we reached the dock. I lifted her onboard the *Victoria Marie*. "We're going on a fun adventure. You love adventures, don't you?"

She smiled and nodded, and I hoisted our bags onto the deck before jumping on myself.

"Go sit quietly and dream of where you'd like me to take you. A fairyland?"

"Oh, yes," she said and clapped her hands.

I expected her to ask if Daddy would come, too. I even had a response ready—*he might, at some point, sweetheart*—to soothe her anxieties until we were safely away and I could deal with that problem later. But she didn't ask, and it thrilled me that she was happy to be with me and me alone.

I pulled on a sailor's cap, tugged on leather gloves, and told her again to sit quietly and not to move anywhere or the sea monsters would find her. I told her we'd be having a great old time and by day's end, we would be in a magical new town with beautiful rooms and wonderful food.

Then, just as I had seen Jay do the day I'd watched him across the Sound without knowing who he was, I hoisted the sail before we were fully under way. But unlike him that day, I was prepared as the wind caught the sheets and puffed their breath of life into them, as the boat tilted and rushed forward. In a flash, I steered us to open water, feeling with every bouncing wave, every giggle from Pamela, a sense of freedom and youth and determination. Just as I had felt diving into the Sound. One, long, glorious exhale of liberation.

I tacked so that we caught every bit of wind, and we raced across the water as if I were in a competition. At last, I felt no fear.

I could see our house and the road as we glided away. Just before it faded from view, I caught sight of the black car of Mr. Delacorte's associate creeping up to the gates.

I would never be anyone's little fool again. I'd not be the golden girl. I'd not be the one treated like an object, or a goddess to be used.

My plan was to make port in Delaware or Maryland by day's end, and then perhaps proceed into the Chesapeake Bay. As confident as I felt sailing, I knew I wasn't up to a long ocean journey, so I hugged the south shore. That night, we would nestle into a sweet old inn, and then I would use some cash to buy train tickets west, somewhere far away, somewhere the sun shone for most of the year. But not before selling the boat, and pocketing that cash for the upcoming trip.

As the boat clipped over a large wave late that afternoon, Pammy giggled again, and in her face I saw a reflection of who I used to be—open to the world, confident of everyone's love, and sure that no one would hurt me.

And then I sailed on, in a boat against the current, moving relentlessly toward the future.

EPILOGUE

This is where Nick's recounting ends, but I'm a woman, and so I'll have the last word.

Nick ended our story in a romantic way—the beautiful heroine together again with her original hero, her husband (even if he didn't paint us in the most flattering of tones) after tragedy occurs. Nick was a romantic, and I think, despite his role in bringing Jay and me together, he wanted to believe that I'd make my marriage with Tom work out well, that it could return to some blissful union, strengthened by the drama we'd gone through. So he wrote it that way.

That wasn't to be. I didn't stay with my "hero." He was no hero at all.

For a long time I barely talked to Nick once he wrote our story. After all, he made me a murderer in it, running down "poor" Myrtle Wilson. Of course he made me the villain, the hare-brained, foolish woman, so feckless she's not even aware of the destruction in her wake and careless about it all after she hears what she wrought.

I was no such thing. When his story became a success, Nick refused to tinker with the denouement, and convinced me for a while that if the money helped me, it was best to leave it alone. He published it as a novel, after all, not a work of non-fiction.

Tom's death was the finale in that summer story, though, and he met it in the same way his mistress met hers.

If Mr. Delacorte's "associate" drove up to the house the day I left, he didn't fulfill the contract then, maybe because there were too many people about. All I know is that one day in New York, Tom stepped off a curb or was pushed or tripped, and fell in front of a taxi. So he died as his mistress had, crushed under the wheels of a shiny machine, one he might have even called a "circus car" since it was a bright lavender vehicle, one of the newest of the fleet.

Nick gave me the news. I called him once we'd gotten settled, and asked he not let Tom know where I was, but I needed some help with the very last of the bonds I'd bought through him and not cashed out.

He told me I had no worries about Tom anymore. Tom was dead. I expected to feel less sad than I did, but I wept at the news. He had been my husband, after all, and was Pamela's father. I think I cried longer for him than for Jay. Tom had been more real, our life more substantial, and I cried for what I'd hoped our marriage would be. My time with Jay had been nothing but a dream.

I asked for the details.

"As soon as he realized you were gone, he stopped the move," Nick said. "He didn't figure it out for hours because I guess something went wrong with one of the trucks, and it took a long time to get a new one out to the house."

I could imagine the scene, Tom angry with the movers, supervising the rearrangement of our things once a new truck was brought out, maybe even irritated with me that I wasn't around. I could envision him snapping at servants to go find me.

He called Nick, eventually, demanding to know where I'd headed, but of course, poor Nick didn't know and suggested Tom wait a bit to see if I'd call.

"When he noticed the boat was gone, he was pretty shaken, Daisy, not mad, just quiet. He couldn't believe you'd take Pamela," Nick said, and I wondered if he was deliberately trying to make me feel worse than I did. "He thought maybe you'd taken her out for a short sail to get away from all the mess. Then evening fell, and, well, he knew you weren't coming back. He was worried. I told him to call the police—I didn't know if you'd need help, out in the boat alone—but he didn't want to do that right away."

Of course he wouldn't. Tom might have been shocked I'd left with our daughter, but he wouldn't want to confess to police his wife might have abandoned him, taking his own sloop to do so—it was too embarrassing. So he'd not let anyone know right away that we were gone. He'd want to fix things on his own.

Even if he had headed to the police or coastal forces, they'd not have found our boat. I slipped into our first port in New Jersey and immediately had a new name painted on her stern, something bland, *Calm Waters*. I paid a premium for that quick work but knew it was necessary.

Then Pamela and I had a wonderful day in a fairy palace inn along the shore, with rose-patterned coverlets and china that reminded me of the set Jay had used that first tea we had at Nick's house.

Tom went into the city a few days after I left, Nick said, to hire a private detective to look for me and Pammy. It was there he met his fate, and I don't know if it was at the hands of the Delacorte man or simply bad luck.

I'd not seen the obituary because my life was too filled with deciding my future with Pamela, with arranging for rooms and destinations and travel and all the things I'd relied on men and servants to do for me in the past. I'd not picked up a newspaper for months after leaving Tom.

I was settled by the time I got the news, as I said, and after my grief passed, I set about living a new life, one where I alone was responsible for myself and my daughter.

I wrestled with how to make sure Pamela got her father's inheritance, but that would have meant contacting the estate, and Tom's father was still alive. He was an old-fashioned man, and I had no doubt he might try to take over Pammy's upbringing, perhaps sending me to a madhouse to get me out of the way.

So I did nothing to claim what was rightfully mine and Pammy's. I decided I'd wait a while, and when I felt safe, I'd contact the appropriate lawyers.

The party of those crazy years ended, as you know. The big party of the Roaring Twenties burnt out, the lights were flipped off, celebrants went home, it was over. Everyone became more serious.

In the crash of the stock market that came at decade's end, poor Tom would have faired poorly, so his death saved him that humiliation.

As it turned out, he'd used a good portion of his family's fortune on stocks bought on margin and other dubious deals, all so he wouldn't feel left out of the big money party going on at the time. His was one of the few old rich families to lose everything. No need for me to claim an inheritance now.

His father, I learned later in a newspaper article, ended up killing himself, just as mine had when a jolt in finances had left him hopeless and ashamed. Yes, I eventually figured that out, that my daddy's trip down the stairs had not occurred at all, and that a rope broke his neck, not a fall.

I suspect Jay would have done all right in the tumult. A lot of his money came from bootlegging, which continued as Prohibition crawled into the early part of the next decade. And then I imagine he would have lit on some other wealth-producing plan. He always, always looked to the future.

Nick lost everything in the crash of '29, too, and headed for Hollywood where he worked as a writer for a while, skills he used when penning our tale.

Jordan married well, someone inured against the economic upheaval. She lived in a lovely apartment overlooking Central Park until she met someone else, an actor without a penny to his name. Then her husband divorced her, and she went back to playing golf, having secured a lovely nest egg from her ex-husband when they ended their marriage. She lives near a golf course in the Hamptons now. I'm not sure if she is still with her actor lover. We exchange letters, but Jordan, like Jay, leaves a lot out of her recounting of her life.

As for me...

I was grateful for Nick's investment advice, but more grateful for my own good sense in cashing out as soon as stocks were high as I sought to protect myself and Pammy. I'd even had the sense to sell all my jewelry before it lost its value. It was a risk of a different kind to have all that money on me, but I managed to keep it safe. We lived modestly enough that we never drew attention to ourselves.

After a short stay in Virginia as I contemplated heading west, I sold the boat, and we eventually made our way back home, to Kentucky, where it was my dream to buy back my family homestead.

That was not to be. Beyond my price when I arrived, it sold to some young upstart who made changes and turned it into a boardinghouse. The most I could do was rent some rooms in it for Pammy and me, and I couldn't bring myself to make that move, even though I did go look at quarters there one day, thinking it might be a good choice for us. But to face the heartbreak of being in my lovely old home, where I'd felt safe and feted and loved, seeing it all chopped up with strangers living in the white-and-gold bedroom I used to occupy—that would have been too much to bear.

Instead, we settled into a very small cottage not far from my mother's own similar dwelling, which I decorated with used furniture and sweet little mementoes, having more fun than when I'd had the money to select expensive silverware. This was all mine, not something bestowed on me by a condescending husband or a sweetly obsessed lover. Never once did it feel "shabby" to me.

Pamela asked a few times that first year where Daddy was, and I told her he'd decided to stay in New York. Eventually she stopped asking, and when she was old enough to understand I said he'd been killed in a horrible motor accident shortly before we were supposed to move. She accepted this explanation, and I gave her some photographs of Tom to cherish, so she knew she'd had a loving father.

It was good to be back near my mama. I told her the whole story of that summer, and then she read it anew when Nick's account was published, both of us shaking our heads at what he'd gotten wrong when I pointed out where our stories diverged. After objections on my part, he agreed to share credit, but that, as I already mentioned, eventually faded, even if the royalties came for a short time at least. It was the least he could do since I'd been the one to inspire him to put pen to paper after I'd sent him my own recollections of the tale.

I made my money last for a considerable time before I had to think of supplementing it, and it did come upon me one panicky night after doing numbers at the kitchen table after Pamela's bedtime that I probably had harbored the illusion I'd find and marry another wealthy man who'd raise me back to my former position in life.

It took just that one night to get over that ridiculous notion, and I was determined the very next day to secure a position somewhere.

In some correspondence with Jordan, she suggested I try looking for work at some country clubs and golf courses. Doing what, I asked.

"Dear, you're a pretty face," she wrote. "All you need to do is smile at people and make them feel they're the only ones you care about. It's a talent you've had all your life."

That wasn't much of a duty roster, but I did manage to land a position as a hostess of sorts at a club nearby, greeting people at the door and making sure they knew how to get on the course or find their way to the restaurant on the grounds. It was only a few hours a week—clubs lost a lot of members during those lean years—but it, combined with what was left of my savings, was enough to keep Pammy and me and Mother, who eventually moved in with us, comfortable, and we lived simply and without want for many years. I actually enjoyed the work. I liked meeting people and being nice to them, and they seemed to like me.

Mother passed quietly after contracting pneumonia in the spring of '39, and truth be told, I was glad she didn't live to see horrors visited on Europe again and war come to our very shores.

Pamela turned into a bright young woman, as pretty as I was at that age, with my golden hair and Tom's piercing eyes, a bit taller than I am, and with a fine athletic body and quick, purposeful movements. She always looks as if she has somewhere to go and strides off with the determination of an explorer, even if just to retrieve a notebook from her room.

She had a string of beaux in her high school years she didn't take seriously. She was too serious herself, winning honors at school for writing and swimming. I was so proud of her when she graduated and decided she might even want to go to college.

When she enrolled in Vassar, I worried about how I'd pay for it, but Mother had bought a life insurance policy, unbeknownst to me, and after she passed, I used the proceeds to finance Pamela's education, happy she wouldn't have to work her way through.

Then, the war came, and that's where we are now, with men storming the shores of France to reclaim the battlefields Jay had once helped win.

There's plenty of work at last, and I applied and was accepted at an airplane factory. That money let me buy a new car, and that work with all the women around me who'd been a bit beaten down over the years lifted me up. I finally felt my own life had meaning.

They didn't know me as Daisy Buchanan or even Daisy Fay, my maiden name. I chose to be called Lenore at that time, finally giving myself the romantic moniker I'd always wanted.

I thought I'd be lonely for a man's attention, and over the years there had been a few suitors who called on me, treated me to dinner, but all and all, I was content with my single life, especially now as I work in the factory. None of the luxuries I used to have compares with the radio I was able to buy with a bonus for good work or the money I can send to Pamela from my earnings.

I miss her terribly, but rejoice that she is on her own, able to provide for herself. Jordan sometimes sees her in New York when she herself is there, because Pamela occasionally writes for a magazine.

DAISY

Pamela wrote me she's seeing someone, a soldier named Richard, Richard D'Invilliers or some other ostentatious name, about to go overseas, and she worries about whether he'll be safe, if they should marry before he goes, or if she should wait until he returns.

Thinking of Jay, I started to write to her to wait, that she'd regret not waiting. I tore up that paper and began anew:

Dearest Daughter,

Aunt Jordan says you are doing very well and might be hired as a staff writer soon. You are making your way in the world. I am so proud of you. It's hard for me to advise you on whether you should wait or marry now. Only you know what is best for you and what future you wish to choose. That's the important thing, dear—what you wish to do…

ABOUT *DAISY*

Two novels greatly influenced me as a writer, books I'd first encountered as a girl. One was Charlotte Bronte's *Jane Eyre*, whose sweeping storytelling seduced me from beginning to end. I wished I could tell stories like that.

The other was F. Scott Fitzgerald's *The Great Gatsby*, a shorter and simpler tale, but one whose use of evocative language made me want to be a writer myself. He made you feel as well as understand the story.

It took many years for me to give myself permission to pursue that goal of being a writer, and in the meantime I read virtually all of the Fitzgerald oeuvre and more—his short stories, his novels (including *Trimalchio*, the first draft of *Gatsby*), *The Crack-up*, plus Zelda's book, *Save Me the Waltz*, and numerous biographies of that ill-fated pair.

When I came up with the idea of imagining the Gatsby story from Daisy's point of view, I knew the novel could not be a mere point-by-point retelling of that famous tale. It had to convey something more, something readers either didn't get from the original or felt was missing and would enjoy seeing, a sort of behind-the-scenes look at the story.

This was the approach I used when writing a retelling, *Sloane Hall*, of Bronte's classic. I not only wanted readers to experience that story afresh as if never having read it before. I wanted to expand on Bronte's exploration of characters and themes.

DAISY

In *Gatsby*, I felt called to develop Daisy's character. The original isn't her story—it's Gatsby's, Nick's, even Tom's. I missed her and wanted to get to know her better. In the original, she is like a sprite, something not real, not flesh and blood, a woman two men coveted but whose physicality is something distant or even symbolic, like that green light at the end of her pier. She is a possession, sought after and jealously guarded.

I wanted to make her real and yet not have her lose the romanticism of the original character, her sweet beauty and grace and desirability.

As I explored her character, I came to ponder how hemmed in women's lives were during that period. I am of a generation that knew only some of that imprisonment. Women couldn't get credit cards when I was young, but in Daisy's time—well, it was virtually impossible for a woman in her position to be anything but the "fool" she wishes her daughter was, and how natural it was for a male author to draw this woman's character as something a little unreal. (This is not a criticism of Fitzgerald. He was a creature of his time, and he always treated his wife with respect on the page, idealizing her, while in real life he protected and supported her financially, no matter how difficult.)

That was my springboard for carving out her figure more fully, and as I wrote, she became a cipher no longer, but a fiercely intelligent woman whose heart was open to the deepest kind of love, if she could only find it.

And, because Fitzgerald always seemed to use Zelda as the inspiration for his heroines, my Daisy is part Zelda, too, incorporating pieces of Zelda's story along the way—her romance with a French aviator, her diving off a high cliff into the Mediterranean while Scott trembled with fear, her desire to dance and paint, and, of course, her madness. All of these are folded into this new Daisy.

I hope fans of the original like getting to know this Daisy and are not disappointed.

There are changes to the original story, some small, some large, that I incorporated to move plot along or to be true to the characterizations I was painting. Lovers of *The Great Gatsby* will surely notice them, but I hope will be swept up in this new tale.

I hope all who read this understand I'm not trying to compete with Fitzgerald's masterpiece. I'm just using it as a springboard to answer questions this devoted fan mulled for many years—such as, what was Daisy thinking? I guess in that sense, it's a love note to the original or maybe a piece of fan fiction. However it is classified, I hope it brings readers pleasure and, perhaps, an incentive to revisit the original.

LS

ACKNOWLEDGMENTS

Every time I publish a book, I thank my family, and for good reason. They not only support my writing habit, they encourage it (and me, of course). Lately, as we've all grown older, I've found myself also consulting my children for advice, a reversal of roles from when they were younger and an "advice chair" sat at the ready in my room. Now they are wise beyond their years, and they, along with my husband, have been excellent sounding boards and counselors through this crazy publishing business and other life events. I can't thank them enough.

I also need to thank my outstanding daughter-in-law, Evelyn, who is a wonderful mother to our grandchildren, and whose own marketing efforts on behalf of her freelance work set a high bar for my feeble similar attempts.

Another thank-you goes out to Deborah Nemeth, who saw this manuscript in its early stages and provided first-class editing services to help me get it where it is today.

I also want to once again thank my writing friend Jerri, hundreds of miles away, but always close in spirit. An excellent published author, she, too, has offered me frank counsel and the much-needed cheering when my spirits were low.

Finally, I owe a debt of gratitude to my publisher, Bruce L. Bortz of Bancroft Press. He has been an unflagging supporter and always interested in my latest projects, no matter what they are. Every author should have such an encouraging editor.

ABOUT THE AUTHOR

L ibby Sternberg is an Edgar finalist, a Launchpad Prose Top 50 finalist, and a BookLife quarter finalist twice. She writes historical fiction, women's fiction and more under the names Libby Sternberg and Libby Malin, and one of her romantic comedies was bought for film. Her other retelling of a classic story—a Jane-Eyre reiteration titled *Sloane Hall*—was one of only 14 books highlighted in the Huffington Post on the 200th anniversary of Charlotte Bronte's birth.